THE HORROR AT
CAMP JELLYJAM

Look for other **Goosebumps®** books
by R.L. Stine:

The Abominable Snowman of Pasadena
The Barking Ghost
The Cuckoo Clock of Doom
The Curse of the Mummy's Tomb
Deep Trouble
Egg Monsters From Mars
Ghost Beach
Ghost Camp
The Ghost Next Door
The Haunted Mask
How I Got My Shrunken Head
How to Kill a Monster
It Came From Beneath the Sink!
Let's Get Invisible!
Monster Blood
Night of the Living Dummy
One Day at HorrorLand
Say Cheese and Die!
The Scarecrow Walks at Midnight
A Shocker on Shock Street
Stay Out of the Basement
Welcome to Camp Nightmare
Welcome to Dead House
The Werewolf of Fever Swamp

THE HORROR AT
CAMP JELLYJAM

R.L. STINE

SCHOLASTIC INC.
New York Toronto London Auckland Sydney
Mexico City New Delhi Hong Kong Buenos Aires

The *Goosebumps* book series created by Parachute Press, Inc.

ISBN 0-439-56834-X

12 11 10 9 8 7 6 5 4 3 2 1   3 4 5 6 7 8/0

Printed in the U.S.A.   40

First Scholastic printing, July 1995

Mom pointed excitedly out the car window. "Look! A cow!"

My brother, Elliot, and I both groaned. We had been driving through farmland for four hours, and Mom had pointed out every single cow and horse.

"Look out your side, Wendy!" Mom cried from the front seat. "Sheep!"

I stared out the window and saw about a dozen gray sheep — fat, woolly ones — grazing on a grassy green hill. "Nice sheep, Mom," I said, rolling my eyes.

"There's a cow!" Elliot exclaimed.

Now *he* was doing it!

I reached across the backseat and gave him a hard shove. "Mom, is it possible to explode from boredom?" I moaned.

"BOOOOOOM!" Elliot shouted. The kid is a riot, isn't he?

"I told you," Dad muttered to Mom. "A twelve-year-old is too old to go on a long car trip."

"So is an eleven-year-old!" Elliot protested.

I'm twelve. Elliot is eleven.

"How can you two be bored?" Mom asked. "Look — horses!"

Dad sped up to pass a huge yellow truck. The road curved through high, sloping hills. In the far distance, I could see gray mountains, rising up in a heavy mist.

"There's so much beautiful scenery to admire," Mom gushed.

"After a while, it all looks like some boring old calendar," I complained.

Elliot pointed out of his window. "Look! No horses!"

He doubled over, laughing. He thought that was the funniest thing anyone had ever said. Elliot really cracks himself up.

Mom turned in the front seat. She narrowed her eyes at my brother. "Are you making fun of me?" she demanded.

"Yes!" Elliot replied.

"Of course not," I chimed in. "Who would ever make fun of *you*, Mom?"

"When do you ever stop?" Mom complained.

"We're leaving Idaho," Dad announced. "That's Wyoming up ahead. We'll be up in those mountains soon."

"Maybe we'll see Mountain Cows!" I exclaimed sarcastically.

Elliot laughed.

Mom sighed. "Go ahead. Ruin our first family vacation in three years."

We hit a bump. I heard the trailer bounce behind us. Dad had hooked one of those big, old-fashioned trailers to the back of our car. We had dragged it all over the West.

The trailer was actually kind of fun. It had four narrow beds built into the sides. And it had a table we could sit around to eat or play cards. It even had a small kitchen.

At night, we'd pull into a trailer camp. Dad would hook the trailer up to water and electricity. And we spent the night inside, in our own private little house.

We hit another bump. I heard the trailer bounce behind us again. The car lurched forward as we started to climb into the mountains.

"Mom, how do I know if I'm getting carsick or not?" Elliot asked.

Mom turned back to us, frowning. "Elliot, you never get carsick," she said in a low voice. "Did you forget?"

"Oh. Right," Elliot replied. "I just thought it might be something to do."

"Elliot!" Mom screamed. "If you're so bored, take a nap!"

"That's boring," my brother muttered.

I could see Mom's face turning an angry red. Mom doesn't look like Dad, Elliot, and me. She is blond and has blue eyes and very fair skin,

3

which turns red very easily. And she's kind of plump.

My dad, brother, and I are skinny and sort of dark. The three of us have brown hair and brown eyes.

"You kids don't know how lucky you are," Dad said. "You're getting to see some amazing sights."

"Bobby Harrison got to go to baseball camp," Elliot grumbled. "And Jay Thurman went to sleepaway camp for eight weeks!"

"I wanted to go to sleepaway camp, too!" I protested.

"You'll go to camp *next* summer," Mom replied sharply. "This is the chance of a lifetime!"

"But the chance of a lifetime is so boring!" Elliot complained.

"Wendy, entertain your brother," Dad ordered.

"Excuse me?" I cried. "How am I supposed to entertain him?"

"Play Car Geography," Mom suggested.

"Oh, no! Not again!" Elliot wailed.

"Go ahead. I'll start," Mom said. "Atlanta."

Atlanta ends with an A. So I had to think of a city that starts with an A. "Albany," I said. "Your turn, Elliot."

"Hmmmmm. A city that starts with a Y . . ." My brother thought for a moment. Then he twisted up his face. "I quit!"

My brother is such a bad sport. He takes games too seriously, and he really hates to lose. Some-

4

times he gets so intense when he's playing soccer or softball, I really worry about him.

Sometimes when he thinks he can't win, he just quits. Like now.

"What about Youngstown?" Mom asked.

"What about it?" Elliot grumbled.

"I have an idea!" I said. "How about letting Elliot and me ride in the trailer for a while?"

"Yeah! Cool!" Elliot cried.

"I don't think so," Mom replied. She turned to Dad. "It's against the law to ride in a trailer, isn't it?"

"I don't know," Dad said, slowing the car. We were climbing through thick pine woods now. The air smelled so fresh and sweet.

"Let us!" Elliot pleaded. "Come on — let us!"

"I don't see any harm in letting them ride back there for a while," Dad told Mom. "As long as they're careful."

"We'll be careful!" Elliot promised.

"Are you sure it's safe?" Mom asked Dad.

Dad nodded. "What could happen?"

He pulled the car to the side of the highway. Elliot and I slid out. We ran to the trailer, pulled open the door, and hurried inside.

A few seconds later, the car pulled back onto the highway. We bounced along behind it in the big trailer.

"This is so cool!" Elliot declared, making his way to the back window.

"Do I have good ideas or what?" I asked, following him. He slapped me a high five.

We stared out the back window. The highway seemed to tilt down as we headed up to the mountains.

The trailer bounced and swayed as the car tugged it.

The road tilted up steeper. And steeper.

And that's when all our troubles began.

2

"I win!" Elliot cried. He jumped up and raised both fists in triumph.

"Three out of five!" I demanded, rubbing my wrist. "Come on — three out of five. Unless you're chicken."

I knew that would get him. Elliot can't stand to be called a chicken. He settled back in the seat.

We leaned over the narrow table and clasped hands. We had been arm wrestling for about ten minutes. It was kind of fun because the table bounced every time the trailer rolled over a bump in the road.

I am as strong as Elliot. But he's more determined. A *lot* more determined. You never saw anyone groan and sweat and strain so much in arm wrestling!

To me, a game is just a game. But to Elliot, every game is life or death.

He had won two out of three about five times.

My wrist was sore, and my hand ached. But I really wanted to beat him in this final match.

I leaned over the table and squeezed his hand harder. I gritted my teeth and stared menacingly into his dark brown eyes.

"Go!" he cried.

We both strained against each other. I pushed hard. Elliot's hand started to bend back.

I pushed harder. I nearly had him. Just a little harder.

He let out a groan and pushed back. He shut his eyes. His face turned beet-red. I could see the veins push out at the sides of his neck.

My brother just can't stand to lose.

SLAM!

The back of my hand hit the table hard.

Elliot had won again.

Actually, I let him win. I didn't want to see his whole head explode because of a stupid arm-wrestling match.

He jumped up and pumped his fists, cheering for himself.

"Hey — !" he cried out as the trailer swayed hard, and he went crashing into the wall.

The trailer lurched again. I grabbed the table to keep from falling off my seat. "What's going on?"

"We changed direction. We're heading down now," Elliot replied. He edged his way back toward the table.

But we bumped hard, and he toppled to the floor. "Hey — we're going backwards!"

"I'll bet Mom's driving," I said, holding on to the table edge with both hands.

Mom always drives like a crazy person. When you warn her that she's going eighty, she always says, "That can't be right. It feels as if I'm going thirty-five!"

The trailer was bouncing and bumping, rolling downhill. Elliot and I were bouncing and bumping with the trailer.

"What is their problem?" Elliot cried, grabbing on to one of the beds, struggling to keep his balance. "Are they backing up? Why are we going backwards?"

The trailer roared downhill. I pushed myself up from the table and stumbled to the front to see the car. Shoving aside the red plaid curtain, I peered out through the small window.

"Uh . . . Elliot . . ." I choked out. "We've got a problem."

"Huh? A problem?" he replied, bouncing harder as the trailer picked up speed.

"Mom and Dad aren't pulling us anymore," I told him. "The car is gone."

3

Elliot's face filled with confusion. He didn't understand me. Or maybe he didn't believe me!

"The trailer has come loose!" I screamed, staring out the bouncing window. "We're rolling downhill — on our own!"

"N-n-n-no!" Elliot chattered. He wasn't stuttering. He was bouncing so hard, he could barely speak. His sneakers hopped so hard on the trailer floor, he seemed to be tap dancing.

"OW!" I let out a pained shriek as my head bounced against the ceiling. Elliot and I stumbled to the back. Gripping the windowsill tightly, I struggled to see where we were heading.

The road curved steeply downhill, through thick pine woods on both sides. The trees were a bouncing blur of greens and browns as we hurtled past.

Picking up speed. Bouncing and tumbling. Faster.

Faster.

10

The tires roared beneath us. The trailer tilted and dipped.

I fell to the floor. Landed hard on my knees. Reached to pull myself up. But the trailer swayed, and I went sprawling on my back.

Pulling myself to my knees, I saw Elliot bouncing around on the floor like a soccer ball. I threw myself at the back of the trailer and peered out the window.

The trailer bumped hard. The road curved sharply — but we didn't curve with it!

We shot off the side of the road. Swerved into the trees.

"Elliot!" I shrieked. "We're going to crash!"

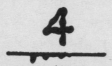

The trailer jolted hard. I heard a cracking sound.

It's going to break in half! I thought.

I pressed both hands against the front and stared out the window. Dark trees flew past.

A hard bump sent me sprawling to the floor.

I heard Elliot calling my name. "Wendy! Wendy! Wendy!"

I shut my eyes and tensed every muscle. And waited for the crash.

Waited . . .

Waited . . .

Silence.

I opened my eyes. It took me a few seconds to realize that we were no longer moving. I took a deep breath and climbed to my feet.

"Wendy?" I heard Elliot's weak cry from the back of the trailer.

My legs were trembling as I turned around. My whole body felt weird. As if we were still bouncing. "Elliot — are you okay?"

He had been thrown into one of the bottom bunks. "Yeah. I guess," he replied. He lowered his feet to the floor and shook his head. "I'm kind of dizzy."

"Me, too," I confessed. "What a ride!"

"Better than Space Mountain!" Elliot exclaimed. He climbed to his feet. "Let's get *out* of this thing!"

We both started to the door at the front. It was an uphill climb. The trailer tilted up.

I reached the door first. I grabbed the handle.

A loud knock on the door made me jump back. "Hey . . . !" I cried.

Three more knocks.

"It's Mom and Dad!" Elliot cried. "They found us! Open it up! Hurry!"

He didn't have to tell me to hurry. My heart skipped. I was so glad to see them!

I turned the handle, pushed open the trailer door —

— and gasped.

5

I stared into the face of a blond-haired man. His blue eyes sparkled in the bright sunlight.

He was dressed all in white. He wore a crisp white T-shirt tucked into baggy white shorts. A small round button pinned to his T-shirt read **ONLY THE BEST** in bold black letters.

"Uh . . . hi," I finally managed to choke out.

He flashed me a gleaming smile. He seemed to have about two thousand teeth. "Hey, guys — everyone okay in there?" he asked. His blue eyes sparkled even brighter.

"Yeah. We're okay," I told him. "A little shaken up, but — "

"Who are *you?*" Elliot cried, poking his head out the door.

The guy's smile didn't fade. "My name is Buddy."

"I'm Wendy. He's Elliot. We thought you were our parents," I explained. I hopped down to the ground.

Elliot followed me. "Where are Mom and Dad?" he asked, frowning.

"I haven't seen anyone, guy," Buddy told him. He studied the trailer. "What happened here? You came unhitched?"

I nodded, brushing my dark hair off my face. "Yeah. On the steep hills, I guess."

"Dangerous," Buddy muttered. "You must have been really scared."

"Not me!" Elliot declared.

What a kid. First, he's shaking in terror and calling out my name over and over. Now he's Mister Macho.

"I've never been so scared in all my life!" I admitted.

I took a few steps away from the trailer and searched the woods. The trees creaked and swayed in a light breeze. The sun beamed down brightly. I shielded my eyes with one hand as I peered around.

No sign of Mom and Dad. I couldn't see the highway through the thick trees.

I could see the tire tracks our trailer had made through the soft dirt. Somehow we had shot through a clear path between the trees. The trailer had come to rest at the foot of a sharp, sloping hill.

"Wow. We were lucky," I muttered.

"You're very lucky," Buddy declared cheerfully. He stepped up beside me, placed his hands

15

on my shoulders, and turned me around. "Check it out. Look where you guys landed!"

Gazing up the hill, I saw a wide clearing between the trees. And then I saw a huge, red-and-white banner, stretched high on two poles. I had to squint to read the words on the banner.

Elliot read them aloud: "King Jellyjam's Sports Camp."

"The camp is on the other side of the hill," Buddy told us, flashing us both a friendly smile. "Come on! Follow me!"

"But — but — " my brother sputtered. "We have to find our parents!"

"Hey — no problem, guy. You can wait for them at the camp," Buddy assured him.

"But how will they know where to find us?" I protested. "Should we leave a note?"

Buddy flashed me another dazzling smile. "No. I'll take care of it," he told me. "No problem."

He stepped past the trailer and started up the hill. His white T-shirt and white shorts gleamed in the sunlight. I saw that his socks and high-tops were sparkling white, too.

That's his uniform. He must work at the camp, I decided.

Buddy turned back. "You guys coming?" He motioned with both hands. "Come on. You're going to like it!"

Elliot and I hurried to catch up to him. My legs

trembled as I ran. I could still feel the trailer floor bouncing and jolting beneath me. I wondered if I would ever feel normal again.

As we made our way up the grassy hill, the red-and-white banner came into clearer view. "King Jellyjam's Sports Camp," I read the words aloud.

A funny, purple cartoon character had been drawn beside the words on the banner. He looked like a blob of grape bubble gum. He had a big smile on his face. He wore a gold crown on his head.

"Who's *that*?" I asked Buddy.

Buddy glanced up at the banner. "That's King Jellyjam," he replied. "He's our little mascot."

"Weird-looking mascot for a *sports* camp," I declared, staring up at the purple, blobby king.

Buddy didn't reply.

"Do you work at the camp?" Elliot asked.

Buddy nodded. "It's a great place to work. I'm the head counselor, guys. So — welcome!"

"But we can't go to your camp," I protested. "We have to find our parents. We have to . . ."

Buddy put a hand on my shoulder and a hand on Elliot's shoulder. He guided us up the hill. "You guys have had a close call. You might as well stay and have some fun. Enjoy the camp. Until I can hook up with your parents."

As we neared the top of the hill, I heard voices. Kids' voices. Shouting and laughing.

17

The clearing narrowed. Tall pine trees, birch trees, and maples clustered over the hill.

"What kind of sports camp is it?" Elliot asked Buddy.

"We play all kinds of sports," Buddy replied. "From Ping-Pong to football. From croquet to soccer. We have swimming. We have tennis. We have archery. We even have a marbles tournament!"

"Sounds like a cool place!" my brother declared, grinning at me.

"Only the best!" Buddy said, slapping Elliot on the shoulder.

I reached the top of the hill first and peered down through the trees to the camp. It seemed to stretch for miles!

I could see two long, white, two-story buildings on either side. Between them, I saw several playing fields, a baseball diamond, a long row of tennis courts, and two enormous swimming pools.

"Those long, white buildings are the dorms," Buddy explained, pointing. "That's the girls' dorm, and that's the boys'. You guys can stay in them while you're here."

"Wow! It looks awesome!" Elliot exclaimed. "Two swimming pools!"

."Olympic size," Buddy told him. "We have diving competitions, too. Are you into diving?"

"Only inside the trailer!" I joked.

"Wendy is into swimming," Elliot told Buddy.

"I think there's a four-lap swim race this afternoon," Buddy told me. "I'll check the schedule for you."

The sun beamed on us as we followed the path down the hill. The back of my neck started to prickle. A cool swim sounded pretty good to me.

"Can anyone sign up for baseball?" Elliot asked Buddy. "I mean, do you have to be on a team or something?"

"You can play any sport you want," Buddy told him. "The only rule at King Jellyjam's Sports Camp is to try hard." Buddy tapped the button on his T-shirt. "Only The Best," he said.

The breeze blew my hair back over my face. I *knew* I should have had it cut before vacation! I decided I'd have to find something to tie it back with as soon as I got into the dorm.

A soccer match was under way on the nearest field. Whistles blew. Kids shouted. I saw a long row of archery targets at the far end of the soccer field.

Buddy started jogging toward the field. Elliot stepped up beside me. "Hey — we wanted to go to camp, right?" he said, grinning. "Well? We made it!"

Before I could reply, he trotted after Buddy.

I brushed back my hair one more time, then followed. But I stopped when I saw a little girl poke her head out from behind a wide tree trunk.

19

She appeared to be about six or seven. She had bright red hair and a face full of freckles. She wore a pale blue T-shirt pulled down over black tights.

"Hey — " she called in a loud whisper. "Hey — !"

I turned toward her, startled.

"Don't come in!" she called. "Run away! Don't come in!"

6

Buddy turned back quickly. "What's the problem, Wendy?" he called.

When I returned my eyes to the tree, the red-haired girl had vanished. I blinked a couple of times. No trace of her.

What was that girl doing out here? I wondered. Did she hide behind that tree just to scare people?

"Uh . . . no problem," I called to Buddy. I followed Elliot and the counselor into the camp.

I quickly forgot all about the girl as we made our way around the soccer field and past a long row of fenced-in tennis courts. The *thwack* of tennis balls followed us as we turned on to the main path that led through the camp.

So many sports! So much activity!

We pushed our way through kids of all ages, eagerly hurrying to the swimming pools, to the baseball diamond, to the bowling lanes!

"Awesome!" Elliot kept repeating. "Totally awesome!"

And for once, he was right.

We passed several other camp counselors. They were all young men and women, dressed completely in white, all of them good-looking and smiling cheerfully.

And we passed dozens of little triangular signs showing the purple, blobby face of King Jellyjam, smiling out from under his shiny gold crown. Under each face was the camp slogan: Only The Best.

He's kind of cute, I decided. I realized I was starting to like *everything* about this amazing sports camp.

And I have to confess I found myself secretly hoping that Mom and Dad wouldn't be able to find Elliot and me for at least a day or two.

Isn't that terrible?

I felt really guilty about it. But I couldn't help thinking it. This camp was just too exciting. Especially after days of riding in the backseat of the car, staring out at cows!

We dropped my brother off at the boys' dorm first. Another counselor, a tall, dark-haired guy named Scooter, greeted Elliot and took my brother off to find a dorm room.

Then Buddy led me to the girls' dorm on the other side of the camp. We passed a gymnastics competition being held in an outdoor arena. Beyond that, one of the swimming pools was jammed with kids watching a diving contest off the high board.

Buddy and I chatted as we walked. I told him about my school and about how my favorite sports are swimming and biking.

We stopped at the white double-door entrance to the dorm. "Where are you from?" I asked him.

Buddy stared back at me. He had such a confused expression on his face. For a moment, I thought he didn't understand the question.

"Do you come from around here?" I asked.

He swallowed hard. He squinted his blue eyes. "Weird . . ." he muttered finally.

"What's weird?" I demanded.

"I . . . I don't remember," he stammered. "I don't remember where I'm from. Is that weird or what?" He raised his right hand to his mouth and nibbled his pointer finger.

"Hey, I forget stuff all the time," I told him, seeing how upset he was.

I didn't get a chance to say anything else. A young woman counselor with very short, straight black hair and bright purple-lipsticked lips came trotting up to us. "Hello. I'm Holly. Are you ready for some sports?"

"I guess," I replied uncertainly.

"This is Wendy," Buddy told her, his expression still troubled. "She needs a room."

"No problem!" Holly declared cheerfully. "Only The Best!"

"Only The Best," Buddy repeated quietly. He flashed me a smile. But I could see he was still struggling to remember where his home was. Weird, huh?

Holly led the way into the dorm. I followed her down a long, white-tiled hall. Several girls came running past, on their way to different sports. They were all shouting and laughing excitedly.

I peeked into some of the open rooms as we passed by them. Wow! I thought. This place is so modern and luxurious! It's not exactly your basic, rustic summer camp.

"We don't stay in the rooms much at all," Holly told me. "Everyone is always outdoors, competing."

She pushed open a white door and motioned for me to step in. Bright sunlight flooded the room from a wide window on the opposite wall.

I saw two bright blue bunk beds against each wall. A sleek white dresser between them. Two white leather armchairs.

The walls were white. They were bare except for a small, framed drawing of King Jellyjam above the dresser.

"Nice room!" I exclaimed, squinting against the bright sunlight.

Holly smiled. Her bright purple lips made the rest of her features seem to disappear. "Glad you like it, Wendy. You can take that bottom bunk over there." She pointed. She had purple finger-nails that matched her lipstick.

"Do I have roommates?" I asked.

Holly nodded. "You'll meet them soon. They'll get you started with some activities. I think they're playing soccer on the lower field. I'm not sure."

She started out of the room, but turned at the doorway. "You'll like Dierdre. I think she's about your age."

"Thanks," I said, gazing around the room.

"Catch you later," Holly replied. She vanished into the hall.

I stood in the center of the sunlit room, thinking hard. What am I supposed to do for clothes? I wondered. What about swimsuits? Sweats?

All I had were the denim short-shorts and pink-and-blue-striped T-shirt I was wearing.

And why didn't Holly tell me where to go next? I asked myself. Why did she just leave me by myself in this empty room?

I didn't have long to ask myself questions.

I started to cross to the window when I heard voices. Whispered voices outside the door.

I turned to the door. Were my roommates returning?

I listened to the excited buzz of whispers.

Then I heard a girl loudly instruct the others. "Come on. We've got her trapped in there. Let's *get* her!"

7

I gasped and searched frantically for a place to hide.

No time.

Three girls burst into the room, their eyes narrowed, their mouths twisted into menacing sneers. They formed a line and moved toward me quickly.

"Whoa! Wait!" I cried. I raised both hands as if to shield myself from their attack.

The tall girl with streaky blond hair was the first to laugh. Then the other two joined in.

"Gotcha," the blond girl declared, tossing back her long hair triumphantly.

I glared back at her, my mouth hanging open.

"Did you really think we were going to attack?" one of the others asked. She was thin and wiry, with very short black hair cut into bangs. She wore gray sweats and a torn gray T-shirt.

"Well . . ." I started. I could feel my face growing hot. Their little joke had really fooled me. I felt like a total jerk.

"Don't look at me," the third girl said, shaking her head. She had frizzy blond hair tumbling out from beneath a blue and red Chicago Cubs cap. "It was all Dicrdre's idea." She pointed to the girl with streaky blond hair.

"Don't feel bad," Dierdre told me, grinning. Her green eyes flashed. "You're the third girl this week."

The other two snickered.

"And did the others think you were attacking?" I asked.

Dierdre nodded, very pleased with herself. "It's kind of a mean joke," she admitted. "But it's funny."

This time I joined in the laughter.

"I have a younger brother. I'm used to dumb jokes," I told Dierdre.

She swept back her hair again. Rummaged around on the dresser top. Found a hair scrunchy to hold it back. "This is Jan and this is Ivy," she said, motioning to the other girls.

Jan was the one with the short black bangs. She slumped on to a lower bunk. "I'm whipped," she sighed. "What a workout. Look at me. I'm sweating like a pig."

"Ever hear of deodorant?" Ivy cracked.

Jan stuck out her tongue at Ivy in reply.

27

"Get changed," Dierdre instructed them both. "We've only got ten minutes."

"Ten minutes till what?" Jan demanded, bending down and rubbing her calf muscles.

"Did you forget the four-lap race?" Dierdre replied.

"Oh, wow!" Jan cried, jumping up. "I *did* forget." She hurried to the dresser. "Where's my swimsuit?"

Ivy followed her. They began frantically sifting through the drawers.

Dierdre turned to me. "Do you want to enter the race?" she asked.

"I — I don't have a swimsuit," I replied.

She shrugged. "No problem. I have about a dozen." She studied me. "We're about the same size. I'm just a little taller."

"Well, I'd *love* a swim," I told her. "Maybe I'll just go to the pool and splash around for a while."

"Huh? Not compete?" Dierdre cried.

All three girls turned to me, stunned expressions on their faces.

"I'll do some sports later," I said. "Right now, I just want to dive in and swim a little. You know. Cool off."

"But — you can't!" Jan cried. She gaped at me as if I had suddenly grown a second head.

"No way," Ivy said, shaking her head.

"You *have* to compete," Dierdre added. "You can't just swim."

28

"Only The Best," Ivy recited.

"Right. Only The Best," Jan agreed.

I felt totally confused. "What do you *mean*?" I demanded. "Why do you keep saying that?"

Dierdre tossed me a blue swimsuit. "Put it on. We're going to be late."

"But . . . but — " I sputtered.

The three girls hurried to get into their swimsuits.

I saw that I had no choice. I went into the bathroom and started to change.

But my questions repeated in my mind. I really wanted them answered.

Why did I have to compete in the race? Why couldn't I just have a swim?

And why did everyone keep repeating "Only The Best"?

What did they mean?

8

The enormous blue pool sparkled under the bright sunlight. The sun hovered high overhead. The concrete burned the soles of my bare feet. I couldn't wait to get into the water.

Shielding my eyes with one hand, I searched for Elliot. But I couldn't find him in the crowd of kids who were waiting to watch the race.

Elliot has probably already played three sports, I told myself. This had to be the perfect camp for my brother!

I gazed down the line of girls waiting to compete in the four-lap race. We all stood on the edge of the deep end of the pool, waiting to jump in.

I silently counted. There were at least two dozen girls in this race. And the pool was wide enough for all of us to have a lane to swim in.

"Hey, you look terrific in my suit," Dierdre said. Her green eyes studied me. "You should have tied your hair back, Wendy. It's going to slow you down."

Wow, I thought. Dierdre really cares about winning.

"Are you a good swimmer?" I asked her.

She swatted a fly on the back of her calf. "The best," she replied, grinning. "How about you?"

"I've never really raced," I told her.

The pool counselors were all young women. They wore white two-piece swimsuits. Across the pool, I saw Holly sitting on the edge of the diving board, talking to another counselor.

A tall, red-haired counselor moved to the edge of the pool and blew her whistle. "Everyone ready?" she called.

We all shouted back that we were ready. Then the long line of girls grew silent. We turned to the pool, leaned forward, and prepared to dive in.

The water shimmered beneath me. The sun burned down on my back and shoulders. I felt about to melt. I couldn't wait to jump in.

The whistle blew. I sprang forward and hit the water hard.

I gasped from the shock of the cold against my hot skin. My arms churned hard as I pulled myself forward.

The splash of thrashing arms and kicking feet sounded like the roar of a waterfall. I dipped my face into the water, feeling the refreshing coldness.

Turning my head, I glimpsed Dierdre a few lengths behind me. She swam in a steady rhythm, her arms and legs moving smoothly, gracefully.

I'm ahead of everyone, I realized, glancing across the pool. I'm winning the race!

With a hard kick, I reached the other end of the pool. I made a sharp turn and pushed off. As I started back to the deep end, the other girls were still approaching the shallow end wall.

I pulled myself harder. My heart started to pound.

I knew I'd win the first lap easily. Then there were three laps to go.

Three laps . . .

I suddenly realized how dumb I was. The other girls were pacing themselves. They weren't swimming full speed because they knew it was a four-lap race.

If I kept swimming this hard, I wouldn't survive two laps!

I sucked in a deep breath, then let it out slowly. Slowly . . . slowly . . .

That was the word of the day.

I slowed my kicking. Shot my arms out and pulled them back slowly. Took long breaths. Long, slow breaths.

As I made my turn and started the second lap, several other swimmers had moved beside me. I caught Dierdre's eye as she swam past.

She never broke her steady rhythm. Stroke. Stroke. Breath. Stroke.

On the other side of Dierdre, I saw Jan swimming comfortably, easily. Jan was so small and light. She seemed to float over the water.

Into the third lap. I kept a few lengths behind Dierdre. I had to concentrate on keeping a slow, even pace. I pretended I was a robot, programmed to swim slowly.

Dierdre turned into the fourth lap a few seconds ahead of me. I saw her expression change as she made her turn. She narrowed her eyes. Her entire face grew tight and tense.

Dierdre really wants to win, I saw.

I wondered if I could catch her. I wondered if I could *beat* her.

I made my turn and put on the speed.

I ignored the aching in my arms.

I ignored the cramp in my left foot.

I thrust myself forward, kicking hard from the waist. My hands cut through the water.

Faster.

I glimpsed Jan fall behind. I saw the disappointment on her face as I passed by.

Pounding, thrusting arms and legs churned the water to froth. The splashing became a roar. The roar nearly drowned out the cheers of the kids watching from around the pool.

My heart thudded so hard, I thought my chest might explode.

My arms ached. They felt as if they each weighed a thousand pounds.

Faster . . .

I pulled up beside Dierdre. Close. So close, I could hear her gasping breaths.

I glimpsed her face, tight with concentration.

She's just like Elliot, I decided. She wants to win so badly.

Lots of times I *let* Elliot win a game. Because he cared about it so much more than I did. And so did Dierdre.

As we neared the wall at the deep end, I let Dierdre pull ahead.

I saw how much it meant to her. I saw how desperate she was to finish first.

What the heck, I thought. There's nothing wrong with coming in second.

I heard the cheers ring out as Dierdre won the race.

I touched the wall, then dipped below the surface. I pulled myself up and grabbed the wall.

My entire body ached and throbbed. I gasped in breath after breath. I shut my eyes and pulled my hair back with both hands, squeezing the water out of it.

My arms were so tired, I could barely pull myself out of the pool. I was one of the last swimmers out.

The others had all formed a circle around Dierdre. I pushed my way into the crowd of girls to see what was happening.

My eyes burned. I brushed water out of them.

I saw the red-haired counselor hand something to Dierdre. Something gold and shiny.

Everyone cheered. Then the circle broke, and the girls all headed in different directions.

I made my way up to Dierdre. "Way to go!" I exclaimed. "I came close. But you're really fast."

"I'm on the swim team at school," she replied. She held up the gold object the counselor had given her.

I could see it clearly now. A shiny gold coin. It had a smiling King Jellyjam engraved on it. I couldn't read the words around the edge of the coin. But I could guess what they were.

"It's my fifth King Coin!" Dierdre declared proudly.

Why is she so excited about it? I wondered. It wasn't a real coin. It probably wasn't even real gold!

"What's a King Coin?" I asked. The coin gleamed in the sunlight.

"If I win one more King Coin, I can walk in the Winners Walk," Dierdre explained.

I started to ask what the Winners Walk was. But Jan and Ivy came running up to congratulate Dierdre. And the three of them all started talking at once.

I suddenly remembered my brother. Where *is* Elliot? I wondered. What has he been doing?

I turned away from Dierdre and the other girls

and started toward the pool exit. But I had only taken a few steps when I heard someone calling my name.

I spun around to see Holly jogging toward me. Her purple-lipsticked lips were knotted in a fretful expression. "Wendy, you'd better come with me," the counselor told me.

My heart skipped. "Huh? What's wrong?" I asked.

"I'm afraid there's a problem," Holly said softly.

9

Something happened to Mom and Dad!

That's the first thought that burst into my head.

"What's wrong?" I cried. "My parents! Are they okay? Are they — "

"We haven't found your parents yet," Holly said. She wrapped a towel around my trembling shoulders. Then she led me to a bench at the side of the pool.

"Is it Elliot?" I cried, dropping down beside her. "What is wrong?"

Holly kept one arm around my shoulders. She leaned close. Her brown eyes stared into mine.

"Wendy, the problem is that you didn't really try very hard to win the race," she said.

I swallowed hard. "Excuse me?"

"I watched you," Holly continued. "I saw you slow your strokes in the last lap. I don't think you tried your best to win."

"But — but — I — " I sputtered.

Holly continued to stare at me without blinking. "Am I right?" she demanded softly.

"I — I'm not used to swimming that far," I stammered. "It was my first race. I didn't think — "

"I know you're new at camp," Holly said, brushing a fly off my leg. "But you know the camp slogan, right?"

"For sure," I replied. "It's everywhere I look! But what does it mean? 'Only The Best!' "

"I guess it's kind of a warning," Holly replied thoughtfully. "That's why I decided to talk to you now, Wendy."

"A warning?" I cried. I felt more confused than ever. "A warning about what?"

Holly didn't reply. She forced a smile to her face and stood up. "Catch you later, okay?"

She turned and hurried away.

I wrapped the towel tighter around my shoulders and started back to the dorm to change. As I walked past the tennis courts, I thought hard about Holly's warning.

Why was it so important for me to win the race?

So that I could be awarded one of those gold coins with the blobby purple king on it?

Why should I care about winning coins? Why couldn't I just play some games, make new friends, and have fun?

Why did Holly say she was giving me a warning? A warning about what?

I shook my head, trying to shake away all these puzzling questions. I'd heard about sports camps from some of my friends back home. Some camps, they said, were really tough. The kids were all serious jock types who wanted to win, win, win.

I guessed this was one of those camps.

Oh, well, I thought, sighing. I don't have to love this camp. Mom and Dad will be here soon to take Elliot and me away.

I glanced up — and saw Elliot.

Sprawled face down on the ground. His arms and legs spread out awkwardly. His eyes closed.

Unconscious.

10

"Ooooh!" I let out a frightened wail.

"Elliot! Elliot!" I dropped down beside him.

He sat up and grinned at me. "How many times are you going to fall for that?" he asked. He started to laugh.

I slugged him in the shoulder as hard as I could. "You creep!"

That made him laugh even harder. It really cracks him up when he makes me look like a jerk.

Why do I always fall for the stupid joke? Elliot pulls it on me all the time. And I always believe he's been knocked out cold.

"I'm never falling for that again. Never!" I cried.

Elliot pulled himself to his feet. "Come watch me play Ping-Pong," he said, tugging my hand. "I'm in the tournament. I'm beating this kid Jeff. He thinks he's good because he puts a spin on his serve. But he's pitiful."

"I can't," I replied. I pulled out of his grasp. "I'm dripping wet. I have to change."

"Come watch," he insisted. "It won't take long. I'll beat him really fast, okay?"

"Elliot — " He certainly was excited.

"If I beat Jeff, I win a King Coin," he announced. "Then I'm going to win five more. I want to win six so I can walk in the Winners Walk before Mom and Dad come for us."

"Good luck," I mumbled, rubbing my wet hair with the towel.

"Were you in a swim race? Did you win?" Elliot asked, tugging my hand again.

"No. I came in second," I told him.

He snickered. "You're a loser. Come watch me beat this kid."

I rolled my eyes. "Okay, okay."

Elliot pulled me to a row of outdoor Ping-Pong tables. They were shielded from the sun by a broad, white canvas awning.

He hurried up to the table on the end. Jeff was waiting for him there, softly bouncing a Ping-Pong ball in the air with his paddle.

I had pictured a little shrimpy guy that Elliot could beat easily. But Jeff was a *big*, red-faced, blond kid with bulging muscles. He had to be twice the size of my brother!

I took a seat on a white wooden bench across from the tables. Elliot can't beat this big guy, I

41

thought. My poor brother is in for a major defeat.

As they started to play, Buddy came walking over and sat down beside me. He flashed me a smile. "No word from your parents yet," he said. "But we'll find them."

We watched the Ping-Pong match. Jeff did his serve with the special spin. Elliot slammed it back at him.

To my surprise, the match was really even. I think Jeff was surprised, too. His returns became more and more wild. And a lot of his special serves missed the table entirely!

They had already played two games, Buddy told me. Jeff had won the first, Elliot the second. This was the third and deciding match.

The game was a tie at sixteen, then a tie at seventeen and eighteen.

I watched Elliot become more and more intense. He wanted desperately to win. He leaned stiffly over the table, gripping the paddle so tightly, his hand was white.

Sweat poured off his forehead. He began ducking and dodging, groaning with each hit, trying to slam every ball.

The more frantic and wild Elliot became, the calmer Jeff appeared.

The game was a tie at nineteen.

Elliot missed a shot and angrily slammed his paddle against the table.

I could see that he was losing it. I'd seen this

happen to my brother many times before. He could never win if he stayed this intense.

As he held the ball and prepared to serve, I raised two fingers to the sides of my mouth and blew hard. He lowered the paddle when he heard my loud whistle.

That was my signal. I'd used it many times before. It meant, "Cool it, Elliot. Calm down."

Elliot turned and gave me a quick thumbs-up. I saw him take a deep breath. Then another. My whistle signal always helped him.

He raised the ball and served it to Jeff. Jeff sent back a weak return. Elliot smacked it back into the right corner. Jeff swung off balance and missed.

Jeff served the next one. Elliot backhanded it. Very soft. The ball tipped over the net and dribbled several times on Jeff's side.

Elliot had won!

He let out a gleeful cheer and raised his fists in victory.

Jeff angrily heaved his paddle to the ground and stomped away.

"Your brother is good," Buddy said, climbing to his feet. "I like his style. He's intense."

"For sure," I muttered.

Buddy hurried over to award Elliot his King Coin. "Hey, guy — you only need five more," Buddy said, slapping Elliot a high five, then a low five.

"No problem," Elliot bragged. He held the coin up so I could see it. King Jellyjam smiled out at me, engraved on the coin.

Why did the camp pick this silly little blob for a mascot? I wondered again. He looked like a fat hunk of pudding wearing a crown.

"I've got to get changed," I told Elliot.

He slid the gold coin into the pocket of his shorts. "I'm going to find another sport!" he declared. "I want to win another King Coin before tonight!"

I waved good-bye, then started toward the dorm.

I had walked only a few steps when I heard a low rumbling.

Then the ground started to shake.

I froze. Every muscle in my body locked as the rumbling grew louder.

"Earthquake!" I cried.

11

The ground shook hard. The awning over the Ping-Pong tables shook. The tables bounced on the ground.

My knees buckled. I struggled to stay on my feet.

"Earthquake!" I choked out again.

"It's okay!" Buddy called, running toward me. He was right. The rumbling sound faded quickly. The ground stopped shaking.

"That happens sometimes," Buddy explained. "It's no problem."

My heart still thudded in my chest. My legs wobbled as if they were rubber bands. "No problem?"

"See?" Buddy motioned around the crowded camp. "No one pays any attention. It lasts only a few seconds.

I gazed around quickly. Buddy was right again. The kids in the chess tournament in front of the lodge didn't glance up from their chessboards. The kickball game on the field across from the pool continued without a pause.

"It usually happens once or twice a day," Buddy told me.

"But what causes it?" I demanded.

He shrugged. "Beats me."

"But — everything shook so hard! Isn't it dangerous?" I asked.

Buddy didn't hear me. He was already jogging over to watch the kickball game.

I turned and started walking to the dorm. I felt kind of shaky. I could still hear that strange rumbling sound in my ears.

As I pulled open the door to the dorm, I bumped into Jan and Ivy. They both had changed into white tennis outfits, and they both carried tennis rackets over their shoulders.

"What sports have you been playing?"

"Did you win a King Coin?"

"Wasn't that a great swim race?"

"Are you having fun, Wendy?"

"Do you play tennis?"

They both talked at once and shot out half a dozen questions. They seemed really excited. They didn't give me a chance to answer.

"We need more girls for the tennis tournament," Ivy said. "We're having a two-day tournament. Come to the courts after lunch, okay?"

"Okay," I agreed. "I'm not that good, but — "

46

"See you later!" Jan cried. They both hurried away.

Actually, I am a pretty good tennis player. I have a decent serve. And I do all right with my two-handed backhand.

But I'm not great.

Back home, my friend Allison and I always play for fun. We don't try to kill each other. Sometimes we just keep volleying back and forth. We don't even keep score.

I'll enter the tennis tournament, I decided. And if I lose in the first round, it's no big deal.

Besides, I told myself, Mom and Dad will be here any minute. And Elliot and I will have to leave.

Mom and Dad . . . their faces flashed into my mind.

They must be frantic, I realized. They must be worried sick. I hoped they were okay.

I suddenly had an idea.

I'll call home, I decided. I should have thought of this before. I'll call home and leave a message on our answering machine. I'll tell Mom and Dad on the machine where Elliot and I are.

No matter where he goes, Dad checks for phone messages every hour. Mom always makes fun of him for being so nervous about missing a call.

But they'll both be glad to get this message! I told myself.

What a good idea! I congratulated myself.

Now all I needed was a phone.

There *have* to be phones in the dorm, I decided. I searched the small front lobby. But I didn't see any pay phones.

No one at the front desk. No one I could ask.

I peered down a long hallway. Rooms on both sides. No phones.

I tried the other hallway. No pay phones there, either.

Eager to make my call, I turned and hurried back outside. I let out a long sigh of relief when I spotted two pay phones beside the long white dorm building.

My heart pounding, I jogged over to them.

I picked up the phone closest to me. And I started to raise the receiver to my ear —

— when two strong hands grabbed me from behind.

"Get off the phone!" a voice demanded.

12

"Huh?" I shrieked in surprise and dropped the phone. It spun crazily on its cord.

I turned around. "Dierdre! You scared me to death!" I cried.

Her green eyes flashed excitedly. "Sorry, Wendy. I just had to tell you my news! Look!"

She held out her hand. I saw a stack of gold King Coins.

"I just won my sixth coin!" Dierdre declared breathlessly. "Isn't that awesome?"

"I — I guess," I replied uncertainly. I still couldn't figure out why it was such a big deal.

"I'll be in the Winners Walk tonight!" Dierdre exclaimed. "I can't believe I made it!"

"That's great," I told her. "Congratulations."

"Have you won any King Coins yet?" Dierdre asked, still holding out her hand.

"Uh . . . not yet," I replied.

"Well, get going!" Dierdre urged. "Show them what you've got, Wendy. Only The Best!" She flashed me a thumbs-up with her free hand.

"Right. Only The Best," I repeated.

"We'll have a party," Dierdre continued. "In our room. Right after the Winners Walk. Okay? We'll celebrate."

"Great!" I replied. "Maybe we can get a pizza from the mess hall or something."

"Tell Jan and Ivy," Dierdre instructed. "Or I'll tell them. Whoever sees them first! See you later!"

She ran off, holding the six gold coins tightly in her fist.

I realized I was smiling. Dierdre had been so excited, she'd gotten *me* excited. So excited, I forgot about my phone call.

I have to give this camp a chance, I decided. I have to get into the spirit of things and start having some fun. Only The Best! I'm going to *win* that tennis tournament!

We all ate dinner at long wooden tables in the huge mess hall inside the main camp lodge. The long, high-ceilinged room seemed to stretch on forever.

Loud voices and laughter echoed off the walls over the clatter of plates and silverware. Everyone had a story to tell. Everyone wanted to talk about the games of the day.

After dinner, the counselors led us all to the running track. I searched for Elliot. But I couldn't find him in the crowd.

It was a warm, clear night. A pale sliver of a moon floated low over the darkening trees. As the sun set, the sky faded from pink to purple to gray.

When darkness fell, I saw two flickering yellow lights at the far end of the track, moving toward me. As they came near, I could see that they were torches, carried by two counselors.

A blaring trumpet fanfare made us all grow quiet.

I stepped closer to Jan, who stood at my side. "They sure make a big deal of this," I whispered.

"It *is* a big deal," Jan replied, her eyes straight ahead as the torches approached.

"Do we have any food for the party later?" I whispered.

Jan raised a finger to her lips. "Ssshhhh."

Several more torches had been lighted. The yellow balls of light glowed like tiny suns.

I heard a drumroll. Then a loud march blared from the loudspeaker, all trumpets and pounding drums.

We stood in silence as the parade of torches passed by. And, then, in the flickering yellow light, I saw faces. The smiling faces of the kids who had won their sixth King Coin that day.

51

I counted eight kids. Five boys and three girls.

Their gold coins had been strung as necklaces around their necks. The coins caught the light of the torches and made the faces of the winners appear to glow as they marched by.

Dierdre marched second in line. She seemed so happy and excited! Her coins jangled at her throat. Her smile never faded.

Jan and I waved and called to her, but she marched right past.

A counselor's voice suddenly boomed over the loudspeaker: "Let's hear it for our winners who are taking the Winners Walk tonight!"

A deafening cheer rose up from the kids watching the parade. We all clapped and shouted and whistled until the winners had marched past and the final torches had floated out of sight.

"Only The Best!" the voice shouted over the loudspeaker.

"Only The Best!" we all chanted back. "Only The Best!"

That ended the Winners Walk parade. The lights came on. We all scrambled toward the dorms. The boys ran in one direction, the girls in the other.

"The torches were really cool," I said to Jan as we followed the crowd of girls down the path to the dorm.

"I only need two more King Coins," Jan replied.

"Maybe I can win them tomorrow. Are you playing in the softball tournament?"

"No. Tennis," I told her.

"There are too many good tennis players," Jan replied. "It'll be too hard to win a coin. You should play softball, too."

"Well . . . maybe," I replied.

Ivy was already waiting for us in the room. "Where's Dierdre?" she demanded as Jan and I entered.

"We didn't see her," Jan replied.

"Probably hanging out with the other winners," I added.

"I found two bags of tortilla chips, but I couldn't find any salsa," Ivy reported, holding up the bags.

"Do we have anything to drink?" I asked.

Ivy held up two cans of diet Coke.

"Wow! Great party!" Jan exclaimed, laughing.

"Maybe we should invite some girls in from other rooms," I suggested.

"No way! Then we'd have to share the Cokes!" Jan protested.

We all laughed.

The three of us joked and kidded around for about half an hour, waiting for Dierdre. We sat down on the floor and opened one of the bags of tortilla chips.

Without realizing it, we finished off the whole bag. Then we passed around one of the cans of soda.

"Where *is* she?" Jan demanded, glancing at her watch.

"It's nearly time for lights-out," Ivy sighed. "We won't have much time for a party."

"Maybe Dierdre forgot we were having a party," I suggested, crinkling up the tortilla chip bag and tossing it toward the trash basket.

I missed. Basketball is definitely not my sport.

"But the party was her idea!" Ivy replied. She climbed to her feet and started pacing back and forth. "Where can she be? Everyone is inside by now."

"Let's go find her," I said. The words just popped out of my mouth. That happens to me sometimes. I get a bright idea before I know what I'm saying.

"Yes! Let's go!" Ivy eagerly agreed.

"Whoa. Hold it," Jan said, stepping in front of us, blocking our way to the door. "We're not allowed. You know the rules, Ivy. We're not allowed outside after ten."

"We'll sneak out, find Dierdre, and sneak back in," Ivy replied. "Come on, Jan. What could happen?"

"Right. What could happen?" I chimed in.

Jan was outnumbered. "Okay, okay. But I hope we don't get caught," she muttered. She followed Ivy and me to the door.

"What could happen?" I asked myself, leading the way into the empty hall.

"What could happen?" I repeated as we sneaked out the door, into the night.

"What could happen?"

I didn't know it. But the answer to the question was: *A LOT!*

13

The night had grown warmer. And steamier. As I crept out the door, I felt as if I were stepping into a hot shower.

A mosquito buzzed around my head. I tried to clap it between my hands. Missed.

Jan, Ivy, and I edged our way around the side of the building. My shoes slid on the dew-wet grass. Bright spotlights shone down from the trees, lighting the path.

We crept in the shadows.

"Where should we look first?" Ivy whispered.

"Let's start at the lodge," I suggested. "Maybe all of tonight's winners are partying there."

"I don't hear any partying," Jan whispered. "It's so quiet out here!"

She was right. The only sounds I could hear were the steady chirp of crickets and the whisper of the warm wind through the trees.

Keeping in the shadows, we followed the path

toward the lodge. We passed the swimming pool, empty and silent. The water shimmered like silver under the bright spotlights.

It was such a hot, wet night, I imagined myself jumping into the pool with all of my clothes on.

But we were on a mission: To find Dicrdre. No time to think about late-night swims.

Staying close together, we passed the row of Ping-Pong tables. They made me think of Elliot. I wondered what he was doing. Probably tucked into bed.

Like any sensible person.

We were approaching the first row of tennis courts when Ivy suddenly cried out, "Whoa! Get back!" She grabbed me and shoved me hard against the fence.

I heard soft footsteps on the path. Someone humming.

The three of us held our breath as a counselor walked past. He had curly black hair and wore dark blue sunglasses even though it was night. He wore the white T-shirt and white shorts that made up the counselor's uniform.

We pressed our backs against the tennis court fence. "That's Billy," Jan whispered. "He's kind of cute. He's always so happy."

"He won't be too happy if he catches us," Ivy whispered. "We'll be in major trouble."

Humming to himself, snapping his fingers, Billy

walked past us. The path curved around the other side of the tennis courts. I watched him until he disappeared.

I took a deep breath. I hadn't been breathing the whole time!

"Where's he going?" Ivy wondered.

"Maybe he's going to the party at the lodge," I suggested.

"Why don't we ask him?" Jan joked.

"For sure," I muttered.

We checked out the path in both directions. Then we started walking again.

We made our way past the tennis courts. The spotlights in the trees cast long shadows across the path. The shadows shifted and moved as the tree limbs bobbed in the wind. They looked like dark creatures crawling and slithering over the ground.

Despite the heat of the night, I shivered.

It was kind of creepy walking over these moving shadows. I had the feeling one of them might reach up, grab me, and pull me down.

Weird thought, huh?

I turned back in time to see the lights in the dorm windows start to go out. Lights-out.

I tapped Jan on the shoulder. She turned and watched the dorm, too. As the lights all went out, the building seemed to disappear in front of our eyes. It faded into the black of the night sky.

"M-maybe this wasn't such a good idea," I whispered.

Ivy didn't reply. She bit her lower lip. Her eyes were darting around the darkness.

Jan laughed. "Don't wimp out now," she scolded. "We're almost to the lodge."

We cut through the soccer field. The main lodge stood on a low, sloping hill, hidden by wide, old maple and sassafras trees.

We didn't have to climb very far up the hill to see that the lodge was as dark as the dorm.

"No party up there," I whispered.

Ivy sighed, disappointed. "Well, where could Dierdre be?"

"We could try the boys' dorm!" I joked.

They both laughed.

Our laughter was cut short by a loud fluttering sound, very close by.

"What's that?" Ivy cried.

"Ohhh!" I let out a low moan as I raised my eyes and saw them.

The sky was thick with bats. Dozens of black bats.

Fluttering over the spotlights in the old trees. And, then — swooping down to get us!

14

I couldn't help myself. I let out a scream. Then I shielded my face with both hands.

I heard Jan and Ivy gasp.

The fluttering grew louder. Closer.

I could feel the bats' hot breath on the back of my neck. Then I could feel them clawing at my hair, tearing at my face.

I've got a real good imagination when it comes to bats.

"Wendy, it's okay," Jan whispered. She tugged my hands from my face. She pointed. "Look."

I followed her gaze up to the fluttering black wings. The bats were swooping low. But they weren't swooping at us. They were swooping down and landing on the swimming pool at the bottom of the hill.

In the bright spotlights, I could see them dart into the water — for less than a second. Then sweep back up to the sky.

"I — I don't like bats," I whispered.

"Neither do I," Ivy confessed. "I know they're supposed to be good. I know they eat insects and stuff. But I still think they're creepy."

"Well, they won't bother us," Jan said. "They're just taking a drink." She gave Ivy and me a push to get us started down the hill.

We were lucky. Nobody had heard me scream. But we had walked only a few steps when we spotted another counselor coming down the path. I recognized her. She had straight white-blond hair that tumbled down to her waist from under a blue baseball cap.

Without making a sound, all three of us dove behind a tall evergreen shrub and crouched down.

Did she see us?

I held my breath again.

She kept walking.

"Where are these counselors going?" Ivy whispered.

"Let's follow her," I suggested.

"Stay far back," Jan instructed.

We slowly climbed back to our feet. And stepped out from behind the shrub.

And stopped when we heard the low, rumbling sound.

As the rumbling grew louder, the ground began to shake.

I caught the frightened expressions on my two friends' faces. Ivy and Jan were just as scared as I was.

The ground shook harder, so hard that we dropped to our knees. I leaned on all fours, holding on to the grass. The ground trembled and shook. The rumbling became a roar.

I shut my eyes.

The sound slowly faded.

The ground gave a final tremble, then remained still.

I opened my eyes and turned to Ivy and Jan. They started to stand. Slowly.

"I hate when that happens!" Jan muttered.

"What *is* it?" I whispered. I stood up on shaky legs.

"Nobody knows," Jan replied, brushing grass stains off her knees. "It just happens. A few times a day."

"I think we should give up on Dierdre," Ivy said quietly. "I want to go back. To the dorm."

"Yeah. I'm with you," I replied wearily. "We can have our celebration with Dierdre tomorrow."

"She can tell us all about where she was tonight and what she did," Jan said.

"This was a crazy idea," I muttered.

"It was *your* idea!" Jan exclaimed.

"Most of my ideas are crazy!" I replied.

Hiding in the shadows, we made our way down to the path. I gazed toward the pool. The bats had disappeared. Maybe the rumbling sound had scared them back into the woods.

62

The crickets had stopped chirping. The air remained hot, but silent and still.

The only sound was the scrape of our sneakers on the soft dirt path.

And, then — before we could move or hide — we heard someone else's footsteps.

Rapid footsteps. Running hard. Running toward us.

I stopped short when I heard a girl's desperate cry. "Help me! Please — somebody! Help me!"

15

A hot gust of wind shook the trees, making their eerie dark shadows dance.

I leaped back, startled by the girl's terrified cries.

"Help me! Please — !"

She came running around from the side of the tennis courts. She wore tight blue short-shorts and a magenta midriff top.

Her arms were stretched out in front of her. Her long hair flew wildly behind her head.

I recognized her as soon as she burst into view.

The little red-haired girl with all the freckles. The one who had hidden in the woods and warned Elliot and me not to come into the camp.

"Help me!"

She ran right into me, sobbing hard. I threw my arms around her tiny shoulders and held her. "You're okay," I whispered. "You're okay."

"No!" she shrieked. She tugged away from me.

"What's wrong?" Jan demanded. "Why are you out here?"

"Why aren't you in bed?" Ivy added, stepping up beside me.

The little girl didn't answer. Her entire body trembled.

She grabbed my hand and pulled me behind the bushes beside the path. Jan and Ivy followed.

"I'm not okay," she started, wiping the tears off her freckled cheeks with both hands. "I'm not. I — I — "

"What's your name?" Jan asked in a whisper.

"Why are you out here?" Ivy repeated.

I heard the flutter of bat wings again, low overhead. But I stared at the little girl and forced myself to ignore them.

"My name — it's Alicia," the girl replied, sobbing. "We've got to go. Fast!"

"Huh?" I cried. "Take a deep breath, Alicia. You're okay. Really."

"No!" she cried again, shaking her head.

"You're safe now. You're with us," I insisted.

"We're not safe," she cried. "No one. No one here. I tried to warn people. I tried to tell you . . ." Her words were cut off once again by her loud sobs.

"What *is* it?" Ivy demanded.

"What did you try to warn us about?" Jan asked, leaning down to the crying girl.

65

"I — I saw something *terrible!*" Alicia stammered. "I — "

"What did you see?" I asked impatiently.

"I followed them," Alicia replied. "And I saw it. Something horrible. I — I can't talk about it. We just have to run. We have to tell the others. Everyone. We have to run. We have to get away from here!"

She let out a long breath. Her entire body trembled again.

"But *why* do we have to run?" I asked, placing my hands gently on her shoulders.

I felt so bad. I wanted to calm her. I wanted to tell her that everything would be okay. But I didn't know how to convince her.

What had she seen? What had frightened her so much?

Had she had a bad dream?

"We have to go now!" she repeated shrilly. Her red hair was matted to her face by her tears. She grabbed my arm and pulled hard. "Hurry! We've got to run! I saw it!"

"Saw *what?*" I cried.

Alicia had no time to reply.

A dark-haired counselor stepped up in front of the bushes. "Caught you!" he cried.

16

I froze. My entire body went cold.

The counselor's dark eyes flashed in the light of a spotlight. "What are *you* doing out here?" he demanded.

I sucked in a deep breath and started to answer.

But another voice replied before I could. "Kind of nosy, aren't you?" It was another counselor. A woman with short, black hair.

Breathing hard, trying not to make a sound, I ducked lower behind the bushes. My two friends dropped to their knees.

"You aren't following me — are you?" the first counselor teased.

"Why would I follow you? Maybe you're following me!" the woman teased back.

They didn't see us, I realized happily. We were two feet away from them. But they didn't see us behind the bushes.

A few seconds later, the two counselors strolled off together. My friends and I waited a long while, listening hard until we could no longer hear their voices. Then we climbed slowly to our feet.

"Alicia?" I asked. "Are you okay?"

"Alicia?" Ivy and Jan cried.

The little girl had vanished.

We sneaked back into the dorm through a side door. Luckily, there were no counselors patrolling the halls. No one in sight.

"Dierdre — are you back?" Jan called as we stepped into our room.

No reply.

I clicked on the light. Dierdre's bunk remained empty.

"Better turn off the light," Ivy warned. "It's after lights-out."

I clicked the light back off. Then I stumbled toward my bunk, waiting for my eyes to adjust to the darkness.

"Where is Dierdre?" Ivy asked. "I'm a little worried about her. Maybe we should tell a counselor that she's missing."

"What counselor?" Jan asked, slumping onto her bed. "There's no one around. The counselors are all out somewhere."

"I'm sure she's partying somewhere and forgot all about us," I said, yawning. I bent to pull down the covers on my bed.

"What do you think that little girl saw?" Ivy asked, peering out the window.

"Alicia? I think she had a bad dream," I replied.

"But she was so frightened!" Jan said, shaking her head. "And what was she doing outside?"

"And why did she run away from us like that?" Ivy added.

"Weird," I mumbled.

"Weird is right," Jan agreed. Weird is the word of the night. She made her way to the dresser. "I'm getting changed for bed. Big day tomorrow. I've got to win two more King Coins."

"Me, too," Ivy said, yawning.

Jan pulled out a dresser drawer. "Oh, no!" she shrieked. "No! I don't *believe* it!"

17

"Jan — what is it?" I cried.

Ivy and I tore across the room to the dresser.

Jan continued to stare down into the open drawer. "It's so dark," she said. "I opened Dierdre's drawer by mistake. And — and — it's *empty*!"

"Huh?" Ivy and I both uttered our surprise.

Squinting through the dim gray light, I studied the dresser drawer. Totally empty. "Check the closet," I suggested.

Ivy crossed the room in three or four quick strides. She pulled open the closet door.

"Dierdre's stuff — it's all gone!" Ivy declared.

"Weird," I muttered. It was still the word of the night.

"Why would she move out and not tell us?" Jan demanded.

"Where did she go?" Ivy added.

Good question, I thought, staring at the empty closet.

Where did Dierdre go?

*   *   *

Breakfast was the noisiest meal of the day. Spoons clattered against cereal bowls. Orange juice pitchers banged on the long wooden tables.

Voices rang out as if someone had turned up the volume all the way. Everyone talked excitedly about the sports they planned to play today, the games they planned to win.

I had taken the last shower. So Jan and Ivy were already eating breakfast when I made my way into the mess hall.

As I pushed through the narrow aisle between the tables, I searched for Dierdre. No sign of her.

I hadn't slept very well, even though I was really tired. I kept thinking about Dierdre — and about Alicia. And I kept wondering what was taking Mom and Dad so long to get in touch with us.

I spotted Elliot at the end of a table filled with boys about his age. He had a stack of waffles in front of him, and he was pouring dark syrup over them.

"Elliot — what's up?" I called, squeezing through the aisle to get over to him.

My brother didn't bother saying good morning. "I've got a one-on-one tournament this morning," he reported excitedly. "I could win my third King Coin!"

"Thrills and chills," I replied, rolling my eyes. "You haven't heard anything about Mom and Dad, have you?"

71

He stared at me as if he didn't remember who they were. Then he shook his head. "Not yet. Isn't this a great camp? Did we luck out, or what?"

I didn't reply. My eyes were on the next table. I thought I had spotted Dierdre. But it was just another girl with streaky blond hair.

"Have you won any coins yet?" Elliot asked. He had a mouth full of waffle. Syrup dripped down his chin.

"Not yet," I replied.

He snickered. "They should change the camp slogan for you, Wendy. Only The Worst!"

Elliot laughed. The other boys at the table laughed, too.

As I said, Elliot really cracks himself up.

I wasn't in the mood for his lame jokes. My mind was still on Dierdre. "Catch you later," I said.

I squeezed past the table and headed toward the girls' side of the room. Cheers and laughter rang out at a table near the wall. A scrambled-egg tossing battle had broken out. Three counselors rushed to stop it.

Jan and Ivy's table was full. I found an empty space at the next table. I poured myself a glass of juice and a bowl of cornflakes. But I didn't feel too hungry.

"Hey — !" I called out when I saw Buddy walk by. He didn't hear me over the noise, so I jumped up and ran after him.

"Hi. What's up?" He greeted me with a smile.

His blond hair was still wet from the shower. He smelled kind of flowery. Aftershave, I guessed.

"Do you know where Dierdre went?" I demanded.

He narrowed his eyes in surprise. "Dierdre?"

"A girl in my dorm room," I explained. "She didn't come back to the room last night. Her closet is empty."

"Dierdre," he repeated, thinking hard. He raised his clipboard to his face and ran his finger down it slowly. "Oh, yeah. She's gone." His cheeks turned bright pink.

"Excuse me?" I stared up at him. "Dierdre is gone? Where did she go? Home?"

He studied the sheet on his clipboard. "I guess. It just says she's gone." His cheeks darkened from pink to red.

"That's so weird," I told him. "She didn't say good-bye or anything."

Buddy shrugged. A smile spread over his face. "Have a nice day!"

He started toward the counselors' table at the front of the huge room. But I ran after him. I grabbed his arm.

"Buddy, one more question," I said. "Do you know where I can find a little girl named Alicia?"

Buddy waved to some boys across the room. "Go get 'em, guys! Only The Best!" he shouted to them. Then he turned back to me. "Alicia?"

"I don't know her last name. She's probably six

or seven," I told him. "She has beautiful, long red hair and a face full of freckles."

"Alicia . . ." He chewed his bottom lip. Then he raised the clipboard again.

I watched as he ran his finger down the list of names. When his finger stopped, his cheeks turned pink again.

"Oh, yeah. Alicia," he said, lowering the clipboard. He grinned at me. A strange grin. A chilling grin. "She's gone, too."

18

"Jan! Ivy!" I saw them hurrying from the mess hall, and I chased after them. "We've got to talk!" I cried breathlessly.

"We can't. We're late." Jan straightened her bangs with one hand. "If we don't get to the volleyball nets in time, we can't be in the tournament."

"But it's *important*!" I called as they jogged to the doors.

They didn't seem to hear me. I watched them disappear into the morning sunlight.

My heart pounded in my chest. I suddenly felt cold all over.

I caught up with my brother, who was playfully boxing a tall, skinny boy with short blond hair. "Elliot — come here," I instructed. "Just for a minute."

"I can't," he called. "Remember? My one-on-one contest?"

The tall, skinny boy hurried out the door. I stepped in front of Elliot, blocking his path.

"Give me a break!" he cried. "I don't want to be late. I'm going against Jeff. Remember him? I can beat him. He's big, but he's real slow."

"Elliot, something strange is going on here," I said, backing him against the wall. Kids were staring at us as they made their way outside. But I didn't care.

"*You're* the only one who's strange!" Elliot shot back. "Are you going to let me go to the basketball court or not?"

He started to push past me. I pinned his shoulders to the wall with both hands.

"Just give me one second!" I insisted. "There's something wrong with this camp, Elliot." I let go of him.

"You mean the rumbling noises?" he asked, brushing back his dark hair with one hand. "That's just gas under the ground or something. A counselor explained it to me."

"That's not what I'm talking about," I replied. "Kids are disappearing."

He laughed. "Invisible kids? You mean like a magic trick?"

"Stop making fun of me!" I snapped. "It isn't funny, Elliot. Kids are disappearing. Dierdre from my dorm room? She was in the Winners Walk last night. Then she didn't come back to the room."

Elliot's grin faded.

"This morning, Buddy told me she was gone," I continued. I snapped my fingers. "Just like that. And a little girl named Alicia — she disappeared, too."

Elliot's brown eyes studied me. "Kids have to go home *sometime*," he insisted. "What's the big deal?"

"And what about Mom and Dad?" I demanded. "They couldn't have driven very far before they realized the trailer had come loose. Why haven't they found us? Why hasn't the camp found them?"

Elliot shrugged. "Beats me," he replied casually. He dodged past me and started to the door. "Wendy, you're just unhappy because you stink at sports. But I'm having a great time here. Don't mess it up for me — okay?"

"But — but — Elliot — !" I sputtered.

Shaking his head, he pushed the door open with both hands and escaped into the sunlight.

I balled both hands into tight fists. I really wanted to pound him. Why wouldn't he listen to me? Couldn't he see how upset and frightened I was?

Elliot is the kind of kid who never worries about anything. Everything always seems to go his way. So why should he sweat it?

But you'd think he'd be just a *little* worried about Mom and Dad.

Mom and Dad . . .

I had a heavy feeling in my stomach as I made

my way slowly out the door. Had they been in a car accident or something? Is that why they hadn't found Elliot and me yet?

No. Stop making things worse, I scolded myself. Don't let your imagination run away with you, Wendy.

I suddenly remembered my plan to call home. Yes, I decided, I will do that right now. I will call home and leave a message for Mom and Dad on the answering machine.

I stopped in the middle of the path and searched for a pay phone. A group of girls carrying hockey sticks passed by. I heard a long whistle coming from the pool across from the tennis courts. Then I heard the splash of kids diving into the water.

Everyone is having fun, I thought — except me.

I decided to make the call, then find a sport to play. Something to take my mind off all my crazy worries.

I returned to the row of blue and white pay phones at the side of the lodge. I ran full speed and picked up the nearest phone.

I raised the receiver to my ear and started to punch in our number.

Then I cried out in surprise.

19

"*Hi there, Camper!*" boomed a cheerful, deep voice. "*Have a wonderful day at camp. This is King Jellyjam greeting you. Work hard. Play hard. And win. And always remember — Only The Best!*"

"Oh, no!" I cried. "A stupid message — !"

"*Hi there, Camper! Have a wonderful day — *" The tape started to repeat in my ear.

I slammed the receiver down and picked up the next phone.

"*Hi there, Camper! Have a wonderful day at camp.*" The same jolly, booming voice. The same recorded message.

I tried every phone in the row. They all played the same message. None of the phones were real.

Where are the real phones? I wondered. There *have* to be phones that actually work.

I turned away from the lodge and wandered down the dirt path. As I passed the bushes where

79

Jan, Ivy, and I had hid last night, I felt a chill. And thought about Alicia.

Bright sunlight washed over the sloping, grassy hill. I shielded my eyes and watched a black-and-gold monarch butterfly. It fluttered toward a patch of red and pink geraniums.

I walked aimlessly, searching for a telephone. All around, kids were shouting, laughing, playing hard. I didn't really hear them. I was deep into my own troubled thoughts.

"Hey! Hey! Hey!"

My brother's voice startled me into stopping. I blinked several times, struggling to focus.

I saw that I had wandered down to the basketball court. Elliot and Jeff were having their one-on-one basketball competition.

Jeff dribbled the ball. It thudded loudly on the asphalt court. My brother waved both arms in Jeff's face. Made a grab for the ball.

Missed.

Jeff lowered his shoulder. Bumped Elliot out of the way. Dribbled to the basket — and shot.

"Two points!" he cried, grinning.

Elliot scowled and shook his head. "You fouled me."

Jeff pretended not to hear. He was twice as big as Elliot. A big hulk. He could push Elliot all over the court, if he wanted to.

Whatever made Elliot think he could win?

"What's the score?" Jeff demanded, wiping

sweat off his forehead with the back of one hand.

"Eighteen to ten," Elliot reported unhappily. I didn't need twenty guesses to figure out that my brother was losing.

The basketball court was closed off by a mesh-wire fence. I grabbed the fence with both hands, pressed my face up against it, and watched.

Elliot dribbled, moving back, back, giving himself some space. Jeff moved with him, leaning forward, adjusting his basketball shorts with one hand as he moved.

Suddenly, Elliot burst forward, his eyes on the basket. He started his jump, raised his right hand to shoot — and Jeff grabbed the ball away.

Elliot jumped and shot nothing but air.

Jeff dribbled twice. Put up a two-handed layup. *Swish.* The score was twenty to ten.

Jeff won the game a few seconds later. He let out a cheer and slapped Elliot a high five.

Elliot frowned and shook his head. "Lucky shots," he muttered.

"Yeah. For sure," Jeff replied, using the front of his sleeveless blue T-shirt to mop his sweating face. "Hey, congratulate me, man. You're my sixth victim!"

"Huh?" Elliot stared at him, hands pressed against his knees, struggling to catch his breath. "You mean — ?"

"Yeah." Jeff grinned. "My sixth King Coin. I get to march in the Winners Walk tonight!"

"Wow. That's cool," Elliot replied without enthusiasm. "I still have three coins to go."

I had the sudden feeling that I was being watched. I let go of the wire fence and took a step back.

Buddy had been staring at me from the path. His eyes were narrowed, and his mouth was set in a stern, unhappy expression.

How long had he been standing there?

Why did he look so unhappy? His grim expression gave me a chill.

As I turned to him, he stepped forward. His blue eyes stared hard into mine.

"I'm sorry, Wendy," the counselor said softly. "But you have to go."

20

"Excuse me?" I gaped at him. My mouth dropped open.

What was he saying? *Where* did I have to go?

Did he mean I had to go — *like Dierdre and Alicia?*

"You have to go find a sport," Buddy repeated, still speaking softly. His solemn expression didn't change. "You can't stand around watching other kids play. King Jellyjam would never approve of that."

I'd like to *step* on that ugly little blob! I thought angrily. What a stupid name. King Jellyjam. Yuck!

Buddy had just scared me to death. Was he *trying* to frighten me? I wondered.

No, I quickly decided. Buddy doesn't know that I'm upset about things. How could he know?

Buddy hurried on to the basketball court. He slapped Jeff on the back and handed him a gold King Coin. "Way to go, guy!" he cried, flashing

Jeff a thumbs-up. "I'll see you in the Winners Walk tonight. Only The Best!"

Buddy said a few words to my brother. Elliot shrugged a few times. Then he said something that made Buddy laugh. I couldn't hear their words.

When Elliot trotted off to find his next sport, Buddy strode quickly back to me. He put an arm around my shoulders and guided me away from the basketball court.

"I guess you're just not a self-starter, Wendy," he said.

"I guess," I replied. What was I supposed to say?

"Well, I'm going to give you a schedule for today. See if you like it," Buddy said. "First, I have a tennis match lined up for you. You play tennis, right?"

"A little," I told him. "I'm not that great, but — "

"After tennis, come down to the softball diamond, okay?" Buddy continued. "We'll get you on one of the softball teams."

He flashed me a warm smile. "I think you'll have a lot more fun if you join in — don't you?"

"Yeah. Probably," I replied. I wanted to sound more enthusiastic. But I just couldn't.

Buddy led me onto one of the back tennis courts. An African-American girl about my age was warming up by hitting a tennis ball against a backboard.

She turned and greeted me as I approached. "How's it going?"

"Fine," I replied. We introduced ourselves.

Her name was Rose. She was tall and pretty. She wore a purple tank top over black shorts. I saw a silver ring dangling from one ear.

Buddy handed me a racket. "Have fun," he said. "And watch out, Wendy. Rose already has five King Coins!"

"Are you a good tennis player?" I asked, twirling the racket in my hand.

Rose nodded. "Yeah. Pretty good. How about you?"

"I don't know," I told her honestly. "My friend and I always play just for fun."

Rose laughed. She had a deep, throaty laugh that I liked. It made me want to laugh, too. "I *never* play for fun!" she declared.

She told the truth.

We volleyed back and forth for a while, to get warmed up. Rose leaned forward, tensed her body, narrowed her dark eyes — then started slamming the ball back at me as if we were playing the final set of a championship!

She played even harder once we started our match.

I found out very quickly that I was no match

for her. I was lucky to return a few of her serves!

Rose was a good sport about it. I caught her snickering a few times at my two-handed backhand. But she didn't make fun of my pitiful game. And she gave me some really helpful tips as the match continued.

She won in straight sets.

I congratulated her. She seemed really excited about winning her sixth King Coin.

A woman counselor I hadn't seen before appeared on the court and presented the coin to Rose. "See you at the Winners Walk tonight," she said, grinning.

Then the counselor turned to me. "The softball diamond is right over that hill, Wendy." She pointed.

I thanked her and began walking in that direction. "Don't walk — run!" she called. "Let's see some spirit! Only The Best!"

I let out an unhappy groan. I don't think she heard me. Then I obediently started to run.

Why was everyone always rushing me around here? I complained silently. Why can't I go lie down by the pool and work on my tan?

As the softball diamond came into view, I started to cheer up a little. I actually like softball. I'm not much of a fielder. But I'm a pretty good slugger.

The teams, I saw, had boys and girls on them.

I recognized two of the girls from my breakfast table this morning.

One of them tossed me a bat. "Hi. I'm Ronni. You can be on our team," she said. "Can you pitch?"

"I guess," I replied, wrapping my hands around the bat. "Sometimes I pitch after school on the playground."

She nodded. "Okay. You can pitch the first couple of innings."

Ronni called the other kids together and we huddled. We went around the circle, giving our names. Then the kids who didn't have fielding positions chose their spots.

"If we win, do we *all* get King Coins?" a boy with a fake tattoo of an eagle on his shoulder asked.

"Yes. All of us," Ronni told him.

Everyone cheered.

"Don't start cheering yet. We've got to win first!" Ronni exclaimed.

She went around the circle, giving the batting order. Since I was the pitcher, I batted ninth.

But since I had a bat, I decided to take a few practice swings. I stepped away from the others, behind the third base line.

Easing my hands up on the bat, I took a soft swing. I like to choke up pretty high. I'm not very strong, and it gives me a harder swing.

The bat felt pretty good. I took a few more soft swings.

Then I pulled it behind my shoulder — and swung as hard as I could.

I didn't see Buddy standing there.

The bat smacked him hard in the chest.

It made a sickening *thocccck* as it crashed into his ribs.

I let the bat fall from my hands. Then I staggered back. Stunned. Horrified.

21

Buddy's smile faded. He narrowed his blue eyes at me.

He raised a hand and pointed a finger at me.

"I like the way you choke up," he said. "But maybe we could find you a lighter bat."

"Huh?" My mouth hung open. I couldn't move. I stood there, gaping at him. "Buddy — ?"

He picked up the bat from the ground. "Does it feel comfortable? Let me see you swing again, Wendy." He handed the bat to me.

My hands trembled as I took it from him. I kept my eyes on him. Waited for him to cry out. To grab his chest and collapse in a heap on the ground.

"Some of the aluminum bats are lighter," he said. He brushed back his blond hair with one hand. "Go ahead. Swing again."

I took a few shaky steps away from him. I wanted to make sure I didn't hit him again. Then I choked up on the bat and swung.

"How is it?" he asked.

"F-fine," I stammered.

He flashed me a thumbs-up and went to talk to Ronni.

Whoa! I thought. What is the story here?

I swung that bat into his chest, hard enough to break a few ribs. Or at least knock his breath out.

But Buddy didn't even seem to notice!

What is the story here?

I told Jan and Ivy about it at dinner.

Jan snickered. "I guess your swing isn't as hard as you think."

"But it made a horrible sound! Like eggs breaking or something!" I exclaimed. "And he just went on smiling and talking."

"He probably waited until he was out of sight. Then he screamed his head off!" Ivy suggested.

I forced myself to laugh along with my two friends. But I didn't feel like laughing.

It was all too strange.

I mean, *no one* could take a blow like that right in the chest and not even say "Ouch!"

Our team lost by ten points. But after that *thocccck*, who could think about the game?

I glanced across the room to the counselors' table. Buddy sat at one end, talking and laughing with Holly. He seemed perfectly okay.

I kept glancing at him all through dinner. Again and again, I heard the sickening *thocccck* the bat made as it smashed into his chest. I just couldn't get it out of my mind.

I kept thinking about it as we trooped out to the track after dinner for the Winners Walk. It was a windy night. The torches flickered and nearly went out.

The trees around the track shivered and bent. Their branches seemed to reach down for the ground.

The marching music started, and the winners paraded by. Rose waved to me as she passed. I saw Jeff walking proudly near the back of the line, his gold coins jangling around his neck.

After the ceremony, I hurried back to the room and climbed into bed. Too many troubling thoughts whirred around in my brain. I wanted to go to sleep and shut them out.

The next morning at breakfast, Rose and Jeff were gone.

22

I searched for Rose and Jeff. And I searched for my brother all morning. I knew he'd be playing hard at one of the sports. But I walked from the soccer field at one end of the camp to the driving range at the other end, and I didn't see him.

Had Elliot disappeared, too?

The frightening thought kept tugging at my mind.

We've got to get out of this camp!

I kept repeating those words to myself as I made my way along the crisscrossing dirt paths.

King Jellyjam, the little purple blob, grinned at me from the signs posted everywhere. Even his cartoon smile gave me the creeps.

Something was terribly wrong at King Jellyjam's Sports Camp. And the more I walked, my eyes searching every face for my brother, the more frightened I became.

Buddy caught up to me after lunch. He led me back to the softball diamond. "Wendy, you can't leave your team," he said sternly. "Forget yesterday. You still have a chance. If you win today, you guys all win King Coins."

I didn't want any King Coins. I wanted to see my parents. I wanted to see my brother. And I wanted to get *out* of there!

I didn't pitch today. I played left field, which gave me plenty of time to think.

I planned our escape.

It won't be that hard, I decided. Elliot and I will sneak out after dinner when everyone is watching the Winners Walk. We'll make our way down the hill, back to the highway. Then we'll walk or hitchhike to the nearest town with a police station.

I knew the police would find Mom and Dad for us easily.

A simple plan, right? Now all I had to do was find Elliot.

Our team lost the game seven to nine.

I grounded out to end the game. The other kids were disappointed that the team lost, but I didn't really care.

I still hadn't won a single King Coin. As we trotted toward our dorms, I saw Buddy watching me. He had a fretful expression on his face.

"Wendy — what's your next sport?" he called to me.

I pretended I didn't hear him and trotted away.

My next sport is running, I thought unhappily. Running away from this horrible place.

The ground began to rumble and shake as I passed the main lodge. This time, I ignored it and kept walking to the dorm.

I didn't find Elliot until after dinner. I saw him heading out the mess-hall door with two buddies. They were laughing, talking loudly, and bumping each other with their chests as they walked.

"Elliot!" I called, chasing after him. "Hey, Elliot — wait up!"

He turned away from his two friends. "Oh. Hi," he said. "How's it going?"

"Did you forget you have a sister?" I demanded angrily.

He narrowed his eyes at me. "Excuse me?"

"Where have you been?" I asked.

A grin spread over his face. "Winning these," he said. He raised the chain around his neck to show off the gold King Coins he was wearing. "I've got five."

"Awesome," I said sarcastically. "Elliot — we've got to get *out* of here!"

"Huh? Get out?" He twisted up his face, confused.

"Yes," I insisted. "We have to get away from this camp — tonight!"

"I can't," Elliot replied. "No way."

Kids pushed past us, on their way to watch the

Winners Walk. I followed Elliot out the mess-hall door. Then I pulled him off the path, onto the grass at the side of the building.

"You can't leave? Why not?" I demanded.

"Not till I win my sixth coin," he said. He jangled the coin necklace in my face.

"Elliot — this place is dangerous!" I cried. "And Mom and Dad must be — "

"You're just jealous," he interrupted. He jangled the coins again. "You haven't won any — have you!"

I balled my hands into fists. I wanted to strangle him. I really did.

He was such a competitive jerk. He always had to win everything.

I took a deep breath and tried to speak calmly. "Elliot, aren't you at all worried about Mom and Dad?"

He lowered his eyes for a moment. "A little."

"Well, we have to get out of here and find them!" I declared.

"Tomorrow," he replied. "After the track meet in the morning. After I win my sixth coin."

I opened my mouth to argue with him. But what was the point?

I knew how stubborn my brother can be. If he wanted to win that sixth coin, he wouldn't leave till he won it.

I couldn't argue with him. And I couldn't drag him away. "Right after the track meet tomorrow morning," I told him, "we're out of here! Whether you win or lose. Agreed?"

He thought about it. "Okay. Agreed," he said finally. Then he trotted off to find his friends.

Four kids marched in the Winners Walk. As I watched from the sidelines, I thought about the kids I knew who had marched before.

Dierdre. Rose. Jeff . . .

Had they all gone home? Were they picked up by their parents? Were they back home now safe and sound?

Maybe I'm frightening myself for no reason, I thought.

Everyone else in camp seems to be having a great time. Why am I the only worrier?

And then I remembered that I *wasn't* the only worrier.

Alicia's tear-stained face floated into my mind.

What had Alicia seen that had frightened her so much? Why was she desperately trying to warn us to get away?

I'll probably never find out, I told myself.

When the Winners Walk ceremony ended, I didn't feel like going back to the dorm. I knew I couldn't get to sleep. Too many thoughts troubled my mind.

As the other kids made their way to their rooms, I ducked into the deep shadows. Then I sneaked along the path to the sloping hill that led up to the main lodge.

Hiding behind a wide evergreen shrub, I dropped down onto the grass. It was a cool, cloudy night. The air felt heavy and damp.

I raised my eyes to the sky. Clouds covered the stars and the moon. Far in the distance, I could see tiny red lights moving slowly against the blackness. An airplane. I wondered where it was headed.

Crickets began to chirp. The wind rustled my hair.

I gazed up at the starless sky. Trying to relax. Trying to calm myself down.

After a few minutes, I heard voices. Footsteps.

I pulled myself up to my knees and ducked low behind the shrub.

The voices grew louder. A girl laughed.

Carefully, I peered out from between the piney branches. I saw two counselors, walking rapidly along the path that led up the hill.

Behind them, I spotted another group of counselors making their way quickly up the hill. They all seemed to be in a hurry.

I lowered myself behind the shrub and hid in the darkness.

They're heading to the lodge, I decided. Must be some kind of counselors' meeting.

Their white shorts and T-shirts were easy to

see, even on such a dark night. Keeping out of sight, I watched them make their way up the path.

But to my surprise, they didn't go to the lodge. Several yards from the lodge entrance, they turned off the path and ducked into the woods.

Where were they going?

I saw two more groups of counselors make their way into the trees. There must be a hundred counselors at this camp, I realized. And they're all going into the woods tonight.

I waited until I thought all of the counselors had passed by. Then I slowly pulled myself to my feet.

I stared into the woods. But I could see only darkness. Shadows upon shadows.

I ducked back down when I heard two more voices.

Peering through the evergreen branches, I spied Holly and Buddy. They were taking long strides, walking side by side.

I waited till they passed by. Then I jumped up.

Creeping in the deep shadows, I followed them into the woods.

I didn't stop to worry about getting caught. I had to know where the counselors were all going.

Buddy and Holly moved quickly through the woods, pushing tall weeds out of their way, stepping over fallen tree limbs.

To my surprise, a low, white structure came

into view. It appeared to glow dully in the dim light.

The building was built low to the ground. The top was curved.

I squinted at it through the trees. It looks like an igloo, I thought.

What is this strange building? I wondered. Why is it hidden away in the trees?

A dark opening had been cut into the side. Holly ducked into the low entrance. Buddy followed her in.

I waited nearly a minute. Then I stepped up to the opening.

My heart pounded. Such a strange, little building. Round and smooth as ice.

I hesitated. I peered into the entrance, but couldn't see anything inside. I didn't hear any voices.

What should I do? I asked myself.

Should I go in?

Yes.

I took a deep breath and lowered myself into the opening.

23

Three steep steps led down to a dim entryway. A single red light down near the floor gave off the only light.

I stepped into the dark red glow, then stopped and listened.

I could hear voices speaking softly in the next room.

Trailing my hand along the bare, concrete wall, I moved slowly toward the voices. An open doorway came up on my right.

I stopped outside it. Then I slowly, carefully peered in.

I stared into a large, square room. Four torches hanging at the front of the room sent out flickering orange light.

The counselors sat on long wooden benches, facing a low stage. A purple banner hung over the stage. It proclaimed: **ONLY THE BEST.**

It's a little theater, I realized. Some kind of meeting hall.

But why is it hidden away in the woods? And why are the counselors all meeting here tonight?

I didn't have to wait long for my answer.

Buddy stepped on to the small stage. He walked quickly into the flickering orange torchlight. Then he turned to face the audience of counselors.

I crept into the doorway. There were no torches in the back of the hall. It was pitch-black back there.

Walking on tiptoe, I edged my way along the back wall.

The door to a closet of some kind stood open. I ducked into it.

Buddy raised both hands. The counselors instantly stopped talking. They all sat up straight and stared forward at him.

"Time to refresh ourselves," Buddy called out. His voice echoed off the concrete walls.

The counselors sat stiffly. No one moved. No one made a sound.

Buddy pulled a gold coin from his pocket. A King Coin, I figured. It dangled on a long gold chain.

"Time to refresh our minds," Buddy said. "Time to refresh our mission."

He raised the gold coin high. It glowed in the torchlight as he began to swing it. Back and forth. Slowly.

"Clear your minds," he instructed them, speaking softly now. "Clear your minds, as I have cleared mine."

The gleaming gold coin swung slowly back and forth. Back and forth.

"Clear . . . clear . . . clear your minds," Buddy chanted.

He is *hypnotizing* them! I realized.

Buddy is hypnotizing all the counselors. And he's been hypnotized, too!

I took a step forward. I couldn't *believe* what I was seeing and hearing!

"Clear your minds to serve the master!" Buddy declared. "For that is why we are here. To serve the master in all his glory!"

"To serve the master!" the counselors all chanted back together.

Who is the master? I asked myself.

What are they talking about?

Buddy continued chanting out slogans to the crowd of counselors. His eyes were wide. He never blinked.

"We do not think!" he shouted. "We do not feel! We give ourselves up to serve the master!"

And suddenly I had an answer to some of my questions.

Now I knew why Buddy hadn't cried out, hadn't collapsed to the ground when I swung the bat into his chest.

He had hypnotized away all feeling.

He was in some kind of trance. He couldn't feel the bat. He couldn't feel anything.

"Only The Best!" Buddy cried, raising both fists into the air.

"Only The Best!" the counselors all repeated. Their unblinking faces appeared strange, frozen in the flickering orange light.

"Only The Best! Only The Best!"

They all chanted the slogan over and over. Their voices echoed loudly off the walls. Only their mouths moved. Like puppets.

"Only The Best can serve the master!" Buddy shouted.

"Only The Best!" the counselors chanted one more time.

Buddy had been swinging the gold coin over his head during the entire performance. Now he lowered it back into the pocket of his shorts.

The room grew silent.

A heavy silence. An eerie silence.

And then I sneezed.

24

I cupped my hand over my mouth.

Too late.

I sneezed again.

Buddy's mouth opened wide in surprise. He jabbed a finger in the air, pointing at me.

Several counselors jumped to their feet and spun around.

I turned to the door. Could I escape through it before one of them caught me?

No.

No way I could get over there.

My legs were shaking. But I forced myself to move. I backed against the wall.

Why had I stepped so far into the room? Why hadn't I stayed in the safety of the doorway?

"Who's there?" I heard Buddy call. "It's so dark. Who *is* it?"

Good! I thought. He didn't know it was me.

But in seconds, they'd grab me and drag me into the light.

I took another step back. Another.

Darkness fell over me.

I spun around. "Ohh!" I cried out when I saw that I had nearly toppled down a steep stairway.

It wasn't a closet after all.

Black stone steps curved sharply down. Where did they lead?

I couldn't guess. But I had no choice. The steps were my only chance of escape.

I leaned against the wall and plunged down the stairs. My shoes slid on the smooth stones.

I nearly tripped and went sailing head first. But I grabbed the wall and steadied myself as I started to fall.

The stairs curved down. Down.

The air grew hot and sour. I held my breath. The air smelled like sour milk.

A strange, deep moan rumbled up from down below.

I stopped to catch my breath.

Listened hard.

The low moan rolled up the stairway again. A whiff of sour air invaded my nostrils.

I turned back. Was I being followed? Had the counselors seen me escape through the open door?

No. It had been too dark. I didn't hear anyone on the stairs. They weren't following me.

What smelled so bad down below?

I wanted to stop right there. I didn't want to climb down any farther.

But what choice did I have? I knew they'd be searching for me upstairs.

Leaning a hand against the stone wall, I made my way down.

The stairway led into a long, narrow tunnel. I could see pale light at the end of it. Another deep moan rumbled in the distance. The floor shook.

I took a long breath and passed quickly through the tunnel. The air grew hot and damp. My shoes splashed through puddles on the tunnel floor.

Where does this lead? I wondered. Will it take me back outside?

As I neared the end of the tunnel, a whiff of sour air made me choke. I coughed and struggled to stop my stomach from heaving.

What a disgusting smell!

Like decayed meat and rotten eggs. Like garbage left out in the sun for days and days.

I pressed both hands over my mouth. The odor was so strong, I could *taste* it!

I gagged. Once. Twice.

Don't think about the smell! I ordered myself. Think about something else. Think about fresh flowers. Think about sweet-smelling perfume.

Somehow, I calmed my stomach.

Then, pinching two fingers over my nose to

keep the odor out, I stumbled to the end of the tunnel.

I stopped as the tunnel gave way to a huge, brightly lit chamber.

I stopped and stared — at the ugliest, most frightening thing I had ever seen in my life!

25

Squinting into the bright light, I saw dozens of kids with mops, and buckets, and water hoses.

At first, I thought they were cleaning off a giant, purple balloon. Bigger than any balloon in the Thanksgiving Day parade!

But as the water sprayed over it and the mops soaped its sides, the balloon let out a loud groan.

And I realized I wasn't staring at a balloon. It was a creature. And the creature was alive. I was staring at a monster.

I was staring at King Jellyjam.

Not a cute little mascot. But a fat, gross, purple mound of slime, nearly as big as a house. Wearing a gold crown.

Two enormous, watery yellow eyes rolled around in his head. He smacked his fat purple lips and groaned again. Hunks of thick, white goo dripped from his huge, hairy nostrils.

The disgusting odor rolled off his body. Even holding my nose couldn't keep out the sour stench.

He smelled like dead fish, rotting garbage, sour milk, and burning rubber — all at once!

The gold crown bounced on top of his slimy, wet head. His purple stomach heaved, as if an ocean wave was breaking inside him. And he let out a putrid burp that shook the walls.

The kids — dozens of them — worked frantically. They circled the ugly monster. They hosed him down. Scrubbed his body with mops and sponges and brushes.

And as they worked, little round objects rained down on them. *Click. Click. Click.* The little round things clattered to the floor.

Snails!

Snails popping out through King Jellyjam's skin.

I started to gag again when I realized the hideous creature was *sweating snails*!

I staggered back into the tunnel, pressing my hands over my mouth.

How could those kids stand the horrible, sour stench?

Why were they washing him? Why were they working so hard?

I gasped when I recognized some of the kids.

Alicia!

She held a hose with both hands and sprayed King Jellyjam's bulging, heaving stomach. Her red hair was soaked and matted to her forehead. She cried as she worked, bawling loudly.

I saw Jeff. Rubbing a mop up and down on the monster's side.

I opened my mouth to call to Alicia and Jeff. But my breath caught in my throat, and no sound came out.

And then someone came running toward me. Stumbling and staggering. Into the tunnel. Out of the bright light.

Dierdre!

A dripping sponge in one fist. Her streaky blond hair drenched. Her clothes wrinkled and soaked.

"Dierdre!" I managed to choke out.

"Get away from here!" she cried. "Wendy — run!"

"But — but — " I sputtered. "What is happening? Why are you doing this?"

Dierdre uttered a sob. "Only The Best!" she whispered. "Only The Best get to be King Jellyjam's slaves!"

"Huh?" I gaped at her as she trembled in front of me, shivering from the cold water that had drenched her.

"Don't you see?" Dierdre cried. "These are all winners. All six-coin winners. He gets the strongest kids. The best workers."

"But — why?" I demanded.

Snails popped through the creature's skin and clicked as they hit the hard floor. A wave of sour stench blew over us as another rumbling burp escaped his swollen lips.

110

"Why are you all washing him?" I asked Dierdre.

"He — he has to be washed all the time!" Dierdre exclaimed with a sob. "He has to be kept wet. And he can't stand his own smell. So he gets the strongest kids down here. And makes us wash him night and day."

"But, Dierdre — " I started.

"If we stop washing," she continued. "If we try to take a rest, he — he'll *eat* us!" Her entire body shook. "He — he ate three kids today!"

"No!" I cried, gasping in horror.

"He's so disgusting!" Dierdre wailed. "Those horrible snails popping out of his body . . . that putrid smell."

She grabbed my arm. Her hand was wet and cold. "The counselors are all hypnotized," she whispered. "King Jellyjam has total control over them."

"I — I know," I told her.

"Get out of here! Hurry!" Dierdre pleaded, squeezing my arm. "Get help, Wendy. Please — "

An angry roar made us both jump.

"Oh, no!" Dierdre wailed. "He's seen us! It's too late!"

26

The monster let out another roar.

Dierdre loosened her grip on my arm. We both turned toward him, shaking with fright.

He was bellowing at the ceiling, roaring just to keep everyone terrified. His watery yellow eyes were shut. He hadn't seen Dierdre and me — yet.

"Get help!" Dierdre whispered to me. Then she raised the sponge and ran back to her place at King Jellyjam's side.

I froze for a moment. Froze in horror. In disbelief.

Another rumbling burp jolted me from my thoughts and sent me scurrying through the tunnel. At least now I knew why the camp ground shook so often!

The sour stench followed me through the tunnel and back up the curving, stone steps. I wondered if I could ever get rid of it. I wondered if I could ever breathe freely again.

How can I help those kids? I asked myself. What can I do?

I was too terrified to think clearly.

As I ran through the darkness, I could picture King Jellyjam smacking his gross purple lips. I could see him rolling his yellow eyes. And the ugly black snails squeezing out through his skin.

I felt sick as I reached the top of the stairs. But I knew I didn't have time to worry about myself. I had to save the kids who had been forced to be the monster's slaves. And I had to save the rest of the kids in camp — before they became slaves, too.

I poked my head out of the closet door. The four torches still burned at the front of the small theater. But the room was empty.

Where were the counselors? Out searching for me?

Probably.

Where can I go? I asked myself. I can't spend the night in this closet. I have to breathe some fresh air. I have to go somewhere where I can think.

Carefully, I made my way out of the low igloo. Into the starless night. Hiding behind a wide tree trunk, my eyes searched the woods.

Narrow beams of white light from flashlights darted through the trees, over the ground.

Yes, I told myself. The counselors are searching for me.

I backed up, away from the crisscrossing lights. Trying not to make a sound, I crept between the trees and tall weeds, toward the path that led to the lodge.

Can I get to the dorms and warn everyone? I wondered. Will *anyone* believe me? Will there be counselors guarding the dorms? Waiting for me to show up?

I heard voices on the path. I ducked behind a tree and let two counselors pass. Their flashlights made wide circles over the sloping hill.

As soon as they were out of sight, I darted out from the trees. I ran down the hill. Keeping in deep shadows, I made my way past the swimming pool. Past the tennis courts. All dark and silent now.

A clump of tall hedges beside the track would hide me from all sides, I realized. I ducked behind the hedges, gasping for breath. Dropping to my knees, I crawled into their shelter.

I settled myself on the prickly pine needles beneath the hedges. And peered out. Only darkness now.

I took a deep breath. Then another. Such sweet-smelling air.

I've got to think, I told myself. Got to think . . .

Shouting voices startled me awake.
When had I fallen asleep? Where was I?
I blinked several times. Sat up and stretched.

My body felt stiff. My back ached. Every muscle ached.

I gazed around. Discovered I was still hidden inside the hedges. A gray, cloudy morning. The sun trying to burn through the high clouds.

And the voices?

Cheers?

I raised myself up and peered through the hedges.

The track competition! It had just begun. I saw six boys in shorts and T-shirts, leaning forward as they ran around the track. A crowd of kids and counselors cheering them on.

And in the lead?

Elliot!

"No!" I cried hoarsely, my voice still choked with sleep.

I stepped out from the hedges. Made my way across the grass toward the track.

I knew I had to stop him. I couldn't let him win the race. I couldn't let him win his sixth coin. If he did, they'd make Elliot a slave, too!

He ran hard. He pulled far out in front of the other five.

What could I do? *What?*

In my panic, I remembered our signal.

My two-fingered whistle. My signal for Elliot to take it easy.

He'll hear the whistle and slow down, I told myself.

I raised two fingers to my mouth.

I blew.

No sound came out. My mouth was too dry.

My heart thudded in my chest. I tried again.

No. No whistle.

Elliot turned into the last lap. There was no way to stop him from winning now.

27

No way to stop him — unless I beat him there!

With a desperate cry, I plunged forward and started to run to the track.

My shoes pounded the grass. I kept my eyes on Elliot and the finishing line as I ran. Faster. Faster.

If only I could fly!

Loud cheers rang out as Elliot neared the finish. The other five boys were miles behind!

My shoes thudded onto the asphalt track. My chest felt about to burst. It hurt to breathe. My breath came in loud wheezes.

Faster. Faster.

I heard cries of surprise as I raced over the track. I plunged up behind Elliot, reached out both hands — and tackled him from behind.

We both toppled in a heap, rolling over the hard track, onto the grass. The other boys raced past us to the finish line.

"Wendy, you jerk!" Elliot screamed, jumping to his feet.

"I — can't explain now!" I shouted back, struggling to breathe, struggling to stop the aching in my chest.

I scrambled to my feet and pulled Elliot up. He angrily tried to jerk free. "Why'd you do that, Wendy? Why?"

I saw three counselors running toward me.

"Hurry — !" I ordered my brother. I pulled him away. "Just hurry!"

I think he saw the terror in my eyes. I think he realized that tackling him was a *desperate* act. I think he saw how serious I was.

Elliot stopped protesting and started to run.

I led him over the grass. Up the sloping hill by the lodge. Into the woods.

"Where are we going?" he called breathlessly. "Tell me what's happening!"

"You'll see in a minute!" I called back. "Get ready for a really bad smell!"

"Huh? Wendy — have you totally lost it?"

I didn't answer. I kept running. I led the way into the woods. To the igloo-shaped building.

At the low entrance, I turned back to see if we were being followed. I didn't see anyone.

Elliot followed me into the theater. The torches weren't lit. It was pitch-black inside.

Feeling my way along the back wall, I found

118

the closet door. I pulled it open and led the way down the curving stairs.

Halfway down, the sour odor floated up to greet us. Elliot cried out and cupped both hands over his nose and mouth. "It stinks!" His cry was muffled by his hands.

"It gets worse," I told him. "Try not to think about it."

We jogged side by side through the long tunnel. I wished I had time to warn Elliot. I wished I could tell him what he was about to see.

But I was desperate to save Dierdre, Alicia, and the others.

Gasping from the smell, I burst into King Jellyjam's brightly lit chamber. Water from a dozen hoses splashed over the monster's purple body. Kids scrubbed furiously as he sighed and groaned.

I saw the startled horror on my brother's face. But I couldn't worry about Elliot now.

"Hit the floor!" I screamed at the top of my lungs, cupping my hands into a megaphone. "EVERYBODY — HIT THE FLOOR! NOW!"

I had a plan.

Would it work?

28

The monster's watery yellow eyes grew wide with surprise. His bloated lips parted. I could see two pink tongues dart and coil inside his mouth.

A few of the kids dropped their hoses and mops and flattened themselves on the floor. Others turned to stare at me.

"Stop washing him!" I cried. "Put down your hoses and brushes! Stop working! And hit the floor!"

Beside me, Elliot uttered gasping sounds. I glimpsed him struggling to keep the sick smell from overpowering him.

King Jellyjam let out a furious roar as the rest of the kids obeyed my instructions. Thick, white slime dripped from his nose. His two tongues flicked out between his purple lips.

"Get flat!" I screamed to the kids. "Stay down!"

And then I saw the monster raise a fat purple arm. With a disgusting groan, he leaned over. His slimy flesh rippled all over his body as he reached out.

Reached out to grab Alicia!

"Help! He's going to eat me!" Alicia shrieked. She started to get up.

"No!" I shrieked. "Stay down! Stay flat!"

With a terrified cry, Alicia dropped back to the floor.

King Jellyjam swung his fat hand down. Fumbled it over her. Tried to lift the little girl up. Tried again. Again.

But I had figured right! The monster's fingers were too big, too clumsy to pick up anyone who lay flat on the floor.

King Jellyjam tilted his head back and uttered a roar of disgust.

I cupped my hand over my nose as the disgusting odor grew more intense. Snails pop-pop-popped out of his skin. Rolled down his slimy body. Bounced noisily onto the floor.

The monster flailed his arms. He leaned down again and struggled to pick up some other kids.

But they pressed themselves flat on the floor. He couldn't lift them.

He roared again, weaker this time. His eyes rolled wildly in his enormous head.

The smell burned my eyes. It swirled around me, surrounded me in its sour stench.

King Jellyjam grabbed for a hose. Couldn't pick

it up. He slammed his hand into a bucket. Struggled frantically to splash water on himself.

I stood trembling. Watching every move.

My plan was working. I knew it would work. It *had* to work!

The stench grew even stronger. I could taste it. I could smell it on my skin.

King Jellyjam flailed both arms. Frantically, he struggled to wash himself.

His roars became groans. His body began to shake.

I gasped as he narrowed his eyes at me. He raised a swollen purple finger and pointed. Accusing me!

He leaned forward. Reached out.

Swiped out his enormous hand.

I couldn't move. I was too stunned.

I shuddered.

His hand slid over me. And before I could struggle, he began to tighten his slimy, stinking fingers around my body.

29

"Ohhh." I uttered a horrified moan.

The fat, wet fingers tightened. Waves of odor rose up around me.

I held my breath. But the smell was *everywhere*.

The fingers wrapped themselves tighter.

The monster began to lift me off the ground. Raise me toward his gaping mouth. The two tongues darted and flicked.

And then the tongues drooped over his purple lips.

The fingers loosened their grip.

I slid free as King Jellyjam groaned and fell forward. Kids rolled quickly out of the way. King Jellyjam toppled over headfirst.

The gold crown bounced away. The monster's body made a loud *splat* as it spread over the floor.

"*Yes!*" I choked out happily. I was still shaking, still trying to forget the slimy feel of his fingers against my skin. "*Yes!*"

My plan had worked perfectly.

The kids stopped washing — and King Jellyjam suffocated from his own foul smell!

"Are you okay?" Elliot asked in a trembling voice.

I nodded. "Yes. I think I'm going to be fine."

Elliot held his nose. "I'll never complain about Dad's garden fertilizer again!" he declared.

Cheering and shouting, the other kids climbed to their feet.

"Thank you!" Alicia cried, wrapping me in a hug. The others rushed forward to thank me, too.

There were lots of hugs, lots of tears as we made our way up to the theater and then out into the woods.

"We are *out* of here!" I cried happily to Elliot.

But we all stopped at the edge of the woods when we saw the counselors.

They all stood in front of us, dozens of them, side by side in their white shirts and shorts. They had formed a line along the path.

And I could see from the hard expressions set on their faces that they had not come to welcome everyone back.

As I stared from face to face, Buddy stepped forward. He gave a signal to the other counselors. "Don't let them get away!" he cried.

30

The counselors stepped forward, moving in a line. Their expressions remained hard and threatening. They kept their arms at their sides.

They moved stiffly. Like robots. In a trance.

They took two more steps.

Then a shrill whistle broke the silence.

"Stop right there! Everybody freeze!" a man's voice boomed.

I heard another shrill whistle.

I turned to see several blue-uniformed police officers running up the hill.

The counselors shook their heads, blinked, uttered soft cries. They made no attempt to run.

"Where *are* we?" I heard Holly mutter.

"What's happening?" another counselor asked.

They all appeared dazed and confused. The police whistles seemed to have broken the trance that held them.

The other kids and I all cheered happily as the officers swarmed up the hill.

"How did you know we needed help?" I called.

"We didn't," an officer replied. "A horrible smell floated into town. We wanted to find out what was causing it. We followed it here!"

I had to laugh. The same smell that had killed the monster had actually saved us kids.

"We didn't know there was a problem at this camp," an officer announced. "We'll contact your parents as soon as we can."

Elliot and I led the way down the hill. We were so eager to see Mom and Dad!

The counselors muttered to themselves, gazing around, trying to figure out what had happened.

I turned to Buddy as Elliot and I walked past him. "Are you feeling better?" I asked.

He narrowed his blue eyes at me and squinted hard. He didn't seem to be able to focus. "Only The Best," he murmured. "Only The Best."

Elliot and I were never so glad to be home!

"What took you so long to find us?" Elliot demanded.

Mom and Dad shook their heads. "The police checked everywhere, trying to find you two," Dad replied. "They called the camp several times. The counselor who answered the phone told the police that you weren't there."

"We were so worried," Mom said, biting her bottom lip. "So terribly worried. When we found the trailer empty, we didn't know what to think!"

"Well, we're home safe and sound now," I replied with a grin.

"Maybe you two would like to go away to a *real* camp next summer," Dad said.

"Uh . . . no way!" Elliot and I answered together.

Two weeks later, we had a surprise visitor.

I opened the door to find Buddy on the front stoop. His blond hair was neatly brushed. He wore chinos, a blue-and-white-striped sportshirt, and a dark blue tie.

"I'm so sorry about what happened at camp," Buddy said.

I was still too shocked at seeing him to reply. I just held on to the door and gaped at him.

"Is Elliot home?" Buddy asked.

"Hi." Elliot stepped up beside me. "Buddy! What's up?"

"I brought you this," Buddy replied. He reached into his pants pocket and pulled out a gold coin.

"It's a King Coin," he told Elliot. "You earned it, remember? You actually won the race."

Elliot reached out for it. Then stopped. His hand hung in midair.

I knew what my brother was thinking. This would be his sixth King Coin.

Should he take it?

Finally, he grabbed it. "Thanks, Buddy," Elliot said.

Buddy said good-bye and gave us a wave. Elliot and I watched him get into a car and drive away. Then we closed the door behind us.

"Are you sure you should've taken that?" I asked Elliot.

"Why not?" he replied. "That purple monster is dead — right? What could happen?"

Five minutes later, we both smelled the horrible odor at the same time.

"Yuck!" Elliot groaned. He swallowed hard. "Wendy, wh-what's that smell?" he stammered.

"I — I don't know," I replied in a shaky voice.

I heard Mom laugh behind us. We turned to see her standing in the doorway to the kitchen. "What's wrong?" she asked. "I have a pot of brussels sprouts boiling on the stove!"

Add *more*

Goosebumps®

to your collection . . .

Here's a chilling preview of

THE CUCKOO CLOCK OF DOOM

1

"Isn't it great?" Dad gushed. "It's an antique cuckoo clock. It was a bargain. You know that store across from my office, Anthony's Antiques and Stuff?"

We all nodded.

"It's been in the shop for fifteen years," Dad told us, patting the clock. "Every time I pass Anthony's, I stop and stare at it. I've always loved it. Anthony finally put it on sale."

"Cool," Tara said.

"But you've been bargaining with Anthony for years, and he always refused to lower the price," Mom said. "Why now?"

Dad's face lit up. "Well, today I went into the shop at lunchtime, and Anthony told me he'd discovered a tiny flaw on the clock. Something wrong with it."

I scanned the clock. "Where?"

"He wouldn't say. Do you see anything, kids?"

Tara and I began to search the clock for flaws. All the numbers on the face were correct, and both the hands were in place. I didn't see any chips or scratches.

"I don't see anything wrong with it," Tara said.

"Me either," I added.

"Neither do I," Dad agreed. "I don't know what Anthony's talking about. I told him I wanted to buy the clock anyway. He tried to talk me out of it, but I insisted. If the flaw is so tiny we don't even notice it, what difference does it make? Anyway, I really do love this thing."

Mom cleared her throat. "I don't know, dear. Do you think it really belongs in the den?" I could tell by her face that she didn't like the clock as much as Dad did.

"Where else could we put it?" Dad asked.

"Well — maybe the garage?"

Dad laughed. "I get it — you're joking!"

Mom shook her head. She wasn't joking. But she didn't say anything more.

"I think this clock is just what the den needs, honey," Dad added.

On the right side of the clock I saw a little dial. It had a gold face and it looked like a miniature clock. But it had only one hand.

Tiny numbers were painted in black along the outside of the dial, starting at 1800 and ending at 3000. The thin gold hand pointed to one of the numbers: 2003.

The hand didn't move. Beneath the dial, a little gold button had been set into the wood.

"Don't touch that button, Michael," Dad warned. "This dial tells the current year. The button moves the hand to change the year."

"That's kind of silly," Mom said. "Who ever forgets what year it is?"

Dad ignored her. "See, the clock was built in 1800, where the dial starts. Every year the pointed moves one notch to show the date."

"So why does it stop at three thousand?" Tara asked.

Dad shrugged. "I don't know. I guess the clockmaker couldn't imagine the year three thousand would ever come. Or maybe he figured the clock wouldn't last that long."

"Maybe he thought the world would blow up in 2999," I suggested.

"Could be," Dad said. "Anyway, please don't touch the dial. In fact, I don't want anyone touching the clock at all. It's very old and very, very delicate. Okay?"

"Okay, Dad," Tara said.

"I won't touch it," I promised.

"Look," Mom said, pointing at the clock. "It's six o'clock. Dinner's almost —"

Mom was interrupted by a loud gong. A little door just over the clockface slid open — and a bird flew out. It had the meanest bird face I ever saw — and it dove for my head.

I screamed. "It's alive!"

About the Author

R.L. STINE is the author of the series *Fear Street*, *Nightmare Room*, *Give Yourself Goosebumps*, and the phenomenally successful *Goosebumps*. His thrilling teen titles have sold more than 250 million copies internationally — enough to earn him a spot in the *Guinness Book of World Records*! Mr. Stine lives in New York City with his wife, Jane, and his son, Matt.

Goosebumps®

Would You Dare Visit a Place That Ghosts, Mummies, Vampires, and Other Creepy Creatures Call Home?

 GHOULISH GAMES

 BEASTLY BOOKS

 SPOOKY STORIES

www.scholastic.com/ goosebumps/books

THE MONSTER MOB   ACTIVITIES   AUTHOR INFO   AND MORE!

Once you're there, you may never come back.

Fun and Fright,
Day or Night

Goosebumps

____ 0-439-56824-2 Goosebumps: The Abominable
Snowman of Pasadena

____ 0-439-56825-0 Goosebumps: The Barking Ghost

____ 0-439-56826-9 Goosebumps: The Cuckoo Clock of Doom

____ 0-439-56827-7 Goosebumps: The Curse of the
Mummy's Tomb

____ 0-439-56828-5 Goosebumps: Deep Trouble

____ 0-439-56829-3 Goosebumps: Egg Monsters from Mars

____ 0-439-56830-7 Goosebumps: Ghost Beach

____ 0-439-56831-5 Goosebumps: Ghost Camp

____ 0-439-56832-3 Goosebumps: The Ghost Next Door

____ 0-439-56833-1 Goosebumps: The Haunted Mask

____ 0-439-56834-X Goosebumps: The Horror at Camp
Jellyjam

____ 0-439-56835-8 Goosebumps: How I Got My
Shrunken Head

____ 0-439-56836-6 Goosebumps: How to Kill a Monster

____ 0-439-56837-4 Goosebumps: It Came from
Beneath the Sink!

____ 0-439-56838-2 Goosebumps: Let's Get Invisible!

____ 0-439-56839-0 Goosebumps: Monster Blood

____ 0-439-56840-4 Goosebumps: Night of the
Living Dummy

____ 0-439-56841-2 Goosebumps: One Day
at HorrorLand

____ 0-439-56842-0 Goosebumps: Say Cheese and Die!

____ 0-439-56843-9 Goosebumps: The Scarecrow
Walks at Midnight

____ 0-439-56844-7 Goosebumps: A Shocker on
Shock Street

____ 0-439-56845-5 Goosebumps: Stay Out of the
Basement

____ 0-439-56846-3 Goosebumps: Welcome to
Camp Nightmare

____ 0-439-56847-1 Goosebumps: Welcome to
Dead House

____ 0-439-56848-X Goosebumps: The Werewolf
of Fever Swamp

Available Wherever Books Are Sold, or Use This Order Form

Other Series Worth Screaming About...

Garth Nix
The KEYS to the KINGDOM
The key to a house no one can see—and a mystery that must be solved.

Emily Rodda

DELTORA QUEST

A land of magic—and monsters.

Emily Rodda
DELTORA SHADOWLANDS

An epic fight against forces of darkness.

K.A. Applegate
REMNANTS™
The end of the world has come...and gone.

■ SCHOLASTIC

Don't forget to order these awesome series!